Robilly

Pope

Paper

QCA/06/1926

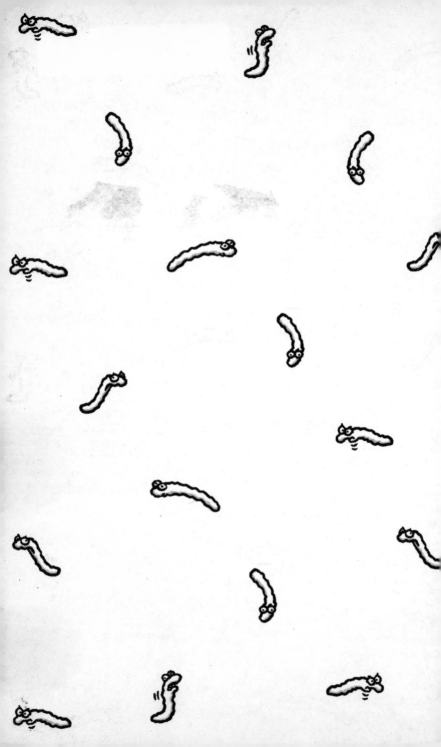

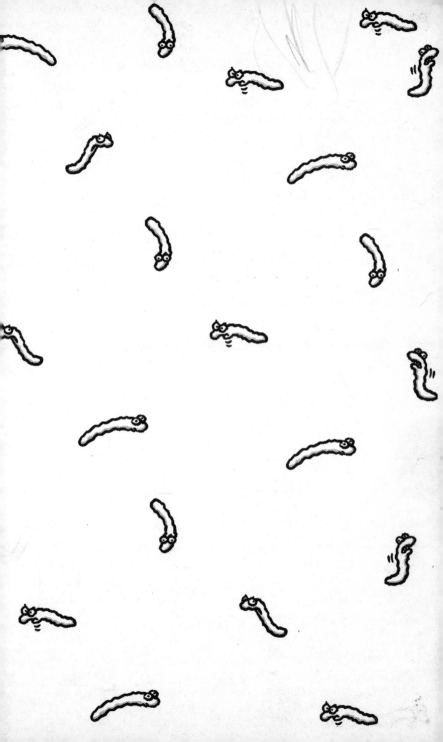

About the author

Michael Lawrence was born at his grandparents' house overlooking a quiet stretch of English river. The house was big and old and ivy-covered, and he was born on the stairs. He's quite glad about this, because if he'd been born fifty metres to the left he'd have started life in the river.

Michael has done several odd things since he first saw the light of day on those stairs. Such as hitch-hike from Amsterdam to Athens in luminous orange boots, scour the country looking for sheep's heads for a travelling circus, sleep in a cardboard box as a penniless down-and-out, and work as an English-language caption-writer for a Japanese public relations firm in Paris. He's also written a number of books and stories for children.

The Jiggy McCue books may be read in any order, but for maximum enjoyment we recommend that they be read in the order in which they were written, which is...

The Poltergoose
The Killer Underpants
The Toilet of Doom
Maggot Pie

ONE FOR ALL AND ALL FOR LUNCH!

Visit Michael at his website: www.wordybug.com

Maggot Pie

ORCHARD BOOKS
96 Leonard Street, London EC2A 4XD
Orchard Books Australia
Unit 31/56 O'Riordan Street, Alexandria, NSW 2015
ISBN 1 84121 756 5
Paperback original
First published in Great Britain in 2002
Text © Michael Lawrence 2002
Illustrations © Ellis Nadler 2002
A CIP catalogue record for this book is available from the British Library.
5 7 9 10 8 6
Printed in Great Britain

Maggot Pie

Michael Lawrence

ORCHARD BOOKS

For Cindy
whose amazing imagination
never fails me when the Ideas Pot
runs a little low

Chapter one

I can hardly bear to tell you this, but I have to tell someone. If I keep it to myself I'll have nightmares about it for the rest of my life, and if there's one thing I don't need in my life it's an extra portion of nightmares. It all started with the stupid genie. If the genie hadn't...

No, that's not right. It actually started with me feeling sorry for myself. Why was I feeling sorry for myself? Because I'm Jiggy McCue, the unluckiest kid in town. I'd never thought of myself as particularly lucky, but just lately luck and me had been complete strangers. I'd been haunted by a dead goose, held prisoner by a pair of evil underpants, and flushed down a computerised toilet. You have to admit, these aren't normal, everyday, run-of-the-mill things to happen to a person. But I had a pretty good idea why I was getting all this stuff thrown at me while it missed everyone else. It was because of what happened at the Piddle Pool the night before I started school for the first time.

What didn't happen, I should say.

The Piddle Pool was called the Piddle Pool because it was a pool people piddled in. Boys anyway. There was this tradition in our town that if a boy weed in the Piddle Pool the night before he started in the Infants he'd have a lucky school life. I don't know what the girls did for luck, never asked, maybe they didn't need it, but boys had been widdling in the Piddle Pool for as long as anybody knew. Smelt like it too. Looked like it. There was always this dirty foamy scum on the surface, and flies all over it, licking their zzz-zzy little lips. It wasn't the sort of pool you wanted to practise the backstroke in.

Where was I? Oh, yes, the night before I started in the Infants. All the boys in my class-to-be at Ranting Lane School had gone to the Piddle Pool with their fathers or older brothers or someone. They stood in a circle round the Pool peeing long and high for luck. It was quite a moment, all those golden arcs falling into the reflected scummy moonlight while proud relatives cheered and the boys grinned happily, knowing they were going to have a really cool time at school.

Every boy except one, that is.

Me.

Because I – I alone – couldn't go.

Maybe it was nerves, having to do it in front of all those others, I don't know. I should have been able to, I'd been saving it up since way before tea. When Dad and I left the house I was cross-legged, thought I'd never make it. But what happens when it's time for the most important pee of my life? Nothing. Not so much as a trickle.

And then everyone was finished and all eyes were on me. On my useless bone dry widget. I didn't know many of the kids yet, so mostly they were strangers' eyes, which made it worse. And then...

'Whassamatter, mate, got a knot in it?'

Those words are embroidered on my heart. They came from almost-five-year-old Bryan Ryan. This was the day we met. The day Ryan became my arch-enemy. If he hadn't said those words the other kids wouldn't have picked up on them and turned them into a chant.

Whassamatter, got a knot?
Whassamatter, got a knot?
Whassamatter, got a knot?
Pee-wee-wee.

And then the water came. Not from where it should though. From a little higher up. My eyes. I turned and ran, followed by jeers and name-calling. My dad came after me, caught me up, walked me home with his hand on my shoulder. And halfway home…

I wet myself.

So that's why I was so unlucky. So I thought anyway. It was also why I'd been secretly sneaking off to the Piddle Pool every chance I got all through my schooldays, and peeing like a maniac in the hope of improving things. Hadn't worked so far, and I didn't have long to make it work. In a matter of days the Piddle Pool would become part of a car park. The car park belonged to the new leisure centre being built on the site of the old brick works. Wouldn't get much luck from peeing on tarmac.

The day my latest batch of troubles started I told Mum I was going to Pete and Angie's and snuck off to the Piddle Pool instead. Nice day. Big fat sun, brilliant blue sky, fluffy-wuffy little clouds. I took up my usual position beside the Piddle Pool. Just across the scummy water was the almost-finished leisure centre. Over to one side was all that was left of the brickworks – three tall thin chimneys that no longer smoked. No one about. I unzipped, flipped out, shut my eyes, got down to business. I'd hardly started when a chilly wind ruffled my hair and pumped my shirt. I opened my eyes. And gasped. Six seconds earlier the world had been all bright and warm. Now it was all gloomy and chilly, and there was a little black cloud parked directly over my head. Then two terrifying things happened, one after the other. First a great puff of purple smoke shot out of one of the dead brickworks chimneys, then lightning sprang from the little black cloud above my head. The lightning struck the Pool right in front of me – kerzoom! kerpow! kerpat! – and the scummy water started churning and bubbling like there was something huge down there that was seriously thinking of leaping out and turning my throat to marmalade. My hair stood on tiptoe, my spine became a jigsaw with a

15

piece missing, and I suddenly thought of several other places I'd rather be. Like my bedroom, with a chair against the door.

I spun round. I picked up my feet. I skedaddled.

To get home from the Piddle Pool I had to pass the library, my school, and Butch & Betty's Unisex Hair Salon. I don't do a lot of running, think it's bad for your health, and I reckoned it must have showed because people kept pointing at me, girls giggled, and a couple of nuns covered their eyes, as if running without practice was a mortal sin or something.

When I shot through the front door of *The Dorks* (our house) the first person I met was Dad, on his way in from the garden for a beer.

'If that was mine I'd put it away, Jig,' he said. 'If your ma sees it she'll probably have you arrested.'

'What are you on about?' I said.

He looked at the front of my jeans. So did I.

And groaned.

No wonder people had pointed. No wonder they'd giggled and covered their eyes. I'd run all the way home from the Piddle Pool with my flies doing an impression of a vertical cat flap on overtime, and everything – the whole kit and caboodle – had been...

No. I can't say it. Just thinking about it makes me sob into my fist.

Chapter Two

Three weeks earlier, Mr Dent our Woodwork teacher had given us a project. 'Construct something,' he said. 'Anything you like, use your imagination.'

'Imagination, sir?' This was me. 'You mean instead of wood?'

'If I had enough wood, Mr McCue,' he replied with a wooden smile, 'I'd use *my* imagination to build an escape-proof cell for you lot.'

'Ah, but then I'd use *my* imagination to escape, wouldn't I?'

'And how would you do that, seeing as I wouldn't have equipped the cell with tools for you to escape *with*?'

'Simple. I'd use Ryan's head as a battering ram. Nothing more wooden than that.'

Ryan snarled at me. I waved some spare fingers at him across the class.

By the end of Week Three most of our projects

were finished. I was quite pleased with mine. Very pleased actually. Mr Dent patted me on the shoulder, and some of the others said nice things. Not Pete though. It would kill Pete to be impressed by anything I do.

'A kennel,' he said. 'Brilliant, seeing as you haven't got a dog.'

'We were told to make something out of wood, not something a dog would live in.'

He held his effort up proudly. 'At least mine's useful.'

'Useful? Pete, it's an ashtray.'

'So?'

'Well for one thing no one in your house smokes. For another it's made of wood. Leave a ciggy smouldering in that and you'll be over a fireman's shoulder before you can burp twice.'

Suddenly there was this great whooping, laughing, cheering sound. A crowd had formed around the benches on the other side of the room. Pete and I went to check it out. Couldn't see a thing till we'd torn some shoulders apart and forced our way through. When we got to the front I immediately wished we'd stayed at the back, because the thing that was getting everyone so worked up was Neil Downey showing off his woodwork project — a little guillotine. The guillotine on its own would have been OK, but Downey was putting it to work, which wasn't so OK. He was executing maggots. He'd brought in a tin of the things, thousands of them, all white and wiggly. No one wanted to touch them, and no one did except Downey, who just dipped in, no gloves, no tweezers, picked one up, dropped it in place. His guillotine had a razor blade on this pulley sort of thing that came down at the flick of a switch. Splat! Maggot in two halves, still wriggling. It was horrible. Disgusting. Downey had never been so popular.

Not with me, though. I have this thing about squiggly-wiggly things. When we were little, Pete would spend hours pulling worms out of the ground to see how far they'd stretch before they snapped. I used to get physically sick just watching. I mean literally throw up. And that was just garden worms. I'd probably turn to a quivering heap of dust if I ever met a snake on a dark night. Spiders, fine. Rats, no big deal. But put me next to a squirmy creature like a snake or a worm – or a maggot – and I almost pass out. I didn't pass out the day Downey brought his tin of maggots in and turned them into small twins, but it was a near thing. I certainly gulped a bit. I grabbed hold of Pete to stop from falling to my knees, but he shook me off. So I dropped to my knees anyway, backed out through all the cheering legs, and staggered over to the window for some lungfuls of pure clean maggotless air.

After school we had to take our woody masterpieces home. No problem for someone with an ashtray or a baby guillotine, less of a breeze for a kennel king. Normally I'd have asked Pete and Angie to help, but Pete had detention for copying my Maths homework error for error, and Angie was at Miss Weeks' Kick-Boxing For Girls Workshop. So I set off alone, kennel on shoulder. I didn't fancy carrying it through the crowded shopping centre, so I did a detour down Effluent Lane. This wasn't a short cut, but there are no shops in Effluent Lane, so you don't see too many people looking for stuff to buy. The kennel was quite heavy and I kept having to stop and put it down, or change shoulders, but in the end I found the best way to carry it was on my back, like a big wooden hump.

I came to the bit of land where the brickworks used to be and the new leisure centre almost was. Passing the Piddle Pool I remembered what happened yesterday. Didn't seem so scary, looking back. Sort of a freak weather thing. Well, the cloud and lightning part. I didn't want to think about the suddenly puffing dead chimney. I decided to take a good-luck leak as I was there. I set the kennel down beside the Piddle Pool, unzipped and took aim. I kept my eyes open this time.

Tinkle, tinkle, tinkle. (That was me.)

'Right. A thousand and one. Here we go.' (That wasn't me.)

You have to picture this. There I am standing on the bank of this stinking old pool, dogless kennel at my side, one hand on hip, the other not, when the stuff I'm peeing into leaps up like a great wave, then comes back down and drenches me all over. I didn't need reminding to zip up this time. Zipped so hard I almost broke my jaw. Then I stood gasping and dripping, wet clothes clinging, yellow piddle scum on the end of my nose. My eyes were waterlogged, so I had to blink hard to see, and what I saw sent me into an immediate jig.* I was no longer alone. A teenager with dreadlocks and no shirt stood waist-deep in the Piddle Pool. And he was speaking.

'Your wish is my command, O...'

He paused after 'O', and his mouth twisted, like his lips were wrestling with one another, but finally said, through his teeth:

'*Master.*'

'What?' I spluttered, jigging around and spitting ancient pee.

'That's you,' he said.

'What's me?'

'You summoned me, which makes me your Humble Servant. Don't let it go to your head, it's just one of those dumb things we have to say. I don't do humble.'

'My servant?' I said, wiping my face on my sleeve.

'I'm a genie,' he said, swiping at some flies. '*Your* genie. That means I have to obey you, like it or not. If I refuse, I go straight back where I came from,

---

* In case you don't know, I wasn't born with the name Jiggy. It's a nickname I got when I was still in my pram. People noticed that whenever I got agitated or nervous or upset my feet started to dance, my fingers twitched, and my elbows flapped. Still happens to this day. Quite a lot actually. Drives some of my teachers up the wall.

and let me tell you I could do with a break from *here.'*

'Whoa,' I said. 'Back up. Genie? You're a genie? *My* genie? You have to obey me? *Me*? Jiggy McCue, unluckiest person on the planet?'

He took a step towards me in the scummy water. I took a step back. Someone who snorkels in urine is more likely to be a dangerous psychopath than a genie.

'Relax,' he said. 'I won't hurt you. I'm here to make your dreams come true. With wishes.'

'W-wishes?' I said, twitching wildly. This was getting serious.

'Wishes. Three. You just won the Piddle Pool lottery, kid.'

He waded to the side and climbed out. I gave him the once-over. Then I gave him the twice-over. He looked about seventeen, and he wasn't just short of a shirt. He wasn't wearing *anything*. I stopped jigging and twitching. So genies came fully equipped, did they?

'Oh, I get it,' I said. 'Some kids from class are setting me up. Ryan? Yeah, probably Bry-Ry. What are you, some pal or sick relative of his?'

The nudist from the Piddle Pool scowled. 'Are you suggesting I'm not what I say I am?'

I said nothing. Just smirked, averted my eyes, dripped quietly.

'You need proof, is that it?' he said.

'What are you gonna do?' I said. 'Conjure up a flying carpet for a grand tour of the ex-brickworks chimneys?'

He mumbled something foreign-sounding and waved a hand. I heard a growl behind me. I jumped. Looked. There was a dog in my kennel. A Rottweiler. In a bad mood.

'Where did that come from?'

'Don't ask me, I'm just the neighbourhood joker,' said the dripping naturist with the dreadlocks.

The Rottweiler came out of the kennel, snapping and snarling at my knees and ankles. I whirled and twisted about, trying to defend myself without actually putting my hands between me and his ferocious jaws.

'It's all right, he's only playing with you,' my new friend said, the way people do seconds before their favourite pet takes your leg off.

'*I am not a toy!!!*' I screamed.

He laughed at this, but he must have done something because the Rottweiler stopped attacking me. Stopped everything, sort of dissolved. Became a little pool of scummy water draining into the earth.

Chapter Three

I panted for a while and tried to get calm while the weirdo from the Piddle Pool admired the view – the heap of rubble that had once been the brickworks.

'You really are a genie,' I said when I'd got some breath back.

'I really am,' he replied.

'You don't talk like a genie. Don't look like one. I mean since when did genies look like teenagers and wear dreadlocks?'

'I can take any form I like. This seemed about right for the time and place.' He looked down at himself. 'I haven't missed anything, have I?'

'Not a thing. Wish you had actually, then I wouldn't have to look the other way all the time. So you're not actually a *teenage* genie?'

'Hardly. If I looked my true age I'd need ten bus passes.'

'But why the Piddle Pool? Don't genies usually hang out in lamps and bottles and things?'

'I didn't choose to live down there. Before a seventeenth-century witch dragged me here, I lived in an urn in Greece – the country, not the melted fat of dead animals.'

'I thought genies were supposed to live in places like Baghdad and serve people like caliphs and sultans and raisins.'

'Raisins?'

'The wives of sultans.'

'The wives of sultans are called sultanas.'

'Oh yeah, I always get those mixed up.'

'You know, it really gets me,' he said. 'Someone tells a handful of stories about a genie from Persia or someplace and the entire world thinks there can't be genies anywhere *but* there.'

'That's true. I never heard of a Greek genie before.'

'I'm not Greek. I just spent a century or so there. I'm originally from Mongolia – Moron.'

'Hey, no need to be rude, how was I to know?'

'Moron,' he said, 'is the provincial capital of Mongolia.'

'It isn't!'

'It is.'

'Oh boy. So if someone didn't like you they could

call you the moron from Moron.'

'Certainly, if they didn't mind their heads being used as cannonballs.'

He didn't seem too pleased. He was glaring at me. I noticed something I'd missed till now.

'Hey. Your eyes.'

'What about them?'

'They're purple. Purple isn't a human eye-colour. If you're going for the full homo sap, here's a tip. Dump the purp. Choose another colour.'

'The eyes are the one thing a genie can't change,' he said. 'Whatever shape or form he takes, so long as it has eyes, they're purple.'

'Tough. Listen, what do you say to putting something on? It's kind of expected to wear clothes this far from a Spanish beach.'

'OK. Soon as I've had a shower.'

He did a Mongolian mutter, flicked a wrist, and a jet of pure clean water fell from absolutely nothing just above his head. He turned round and round in the spray, washing his armpits and a few other pits. Then the water stopped and he stood drying himself in a beam of light. As I was still soaked from head to foot with Piddle Pool water, and smelling pretty bad, I very nearly wasted a wish on a shower and beam of light of my own.

'What sort of clothes should I wear?' he asked when he was done.

'Doesn't matter. Just normal stuff, like me.'

Another mutter, another flick of the wrist, and he was fully dressed. In Ranting Lane school uniform. I let it go.

'You say you're my genie and I summoned you,' I said. 'How does that work? I didn't do any summoning, far as I know.'

'You passed water in my pool a thousand and one times,' he replied, admiring himself in a full-length mirror that hadn't been there a moment before. 'A thousand and one pees is the magic number that makes me all yours. Yesterday, your thousandth, was my wake-up call.'

'The change in the weather, the lightening, the purple smoke from the chimney?'

'I hate being disturbed in my sleep.'

'But I've been widdling here since before my fifth birthday. Are you telling me you've been keeping *count* all this time?'

'There's not a lot else to do down there.' The full-length mirror turned into a fancy high-backed chair with a footstool. The genie sat down and put his feet up. 'You want to get started?'

'Started?'

'On your wishes. I know you humans. Can't wait to get stuck in once you know you can have anything you want for the first time in your pathetic little lives.'

'You don't like us much, do you?'

'You're an inferior species,' he said. 'An inferior species that I have to serve. It's like you having to obey a squirrel. Humiliating. Come on, Wish One.'

'Do I have to do it right away? I mean if this was a fifty-wish deal, no prob, but three, well. Needs thinking about.'

'You people, never grateful. But...' He settled back in his chair, crossed his ankles, closed his eyes. 'I could do with a break from all that water. My brain's starting to wrinkle. No, you take your time.'

'Tell me about the seventeenth-century witch,' I said. 'Like how she brought you here, and why.'

He opened one purple eye. 'Is that of interest to you?'

'No. But it's something to listen to while I think of a wish.'

'Very well.' He closed the eye. 'Back then this was a village pond used for witch-testing. People accused of being witches – females, mostly – were thrown in. If they floated they were witches, if they drowned they weren't.'

'Too late by then to apologise,' I said.

'Just a bit. One day one of the real witches said a genie-conjuring spell as she came up for the fourth time. She may not even have known it was a genie-conjuring spell, but it was, and she got one. Me. All the way from sunny Corfu.'

'Why you? Weren't there any nearer ones?'

'It was the holiday season.'

'So you gave this witch three wishes and she wished to be saved with one of them and you saved her?'

'No, not exactly.'

'What then?'

'They hauled her out of the pool and gagged her and burnt her at the stake before she could wish for anything. Like not to be burnt at the stake.'

'But you didn't have to stay, did you? I mean why didn't you go back to Greece if it was so nice there?'

He opened his eyes. 'The Pool was where she summoned me from, so the Pool was now my home. It's the way it works.'

'And it's because witches were dunked here that people have been peeing here for luck ever since?'

'Yes.' He laughed. 'The things your kind believe in!'

'Hang on, are you saying that if you pee here the night before starting school for the first time you don't get any special luck?'

'That's right. Total hogwash. Complete and utter bummocks.'

'So I've been peeing here for nothing all these years?'

'Except when you were desperate, yes.'

'Well if it's not true, how come I have so much less luck than most other kids?'

'Easy. You're a naturally unlucky person.'

This was bad news. But a look at my watch told me that I didn't have time for more.

'Got to go. If I'm not home from school when my old dear gets in from work her hair turns white.'

'What about the three wishes?' the genie asked.

'Can I get back to you on those?'

'You're the boss. At least till they've been granted.'

'How do I get in touch with you?'

'Just say "I want to make a wish" and I'll appear.'

I hesitated. This was too good to be true. Stuff like this just doesn't happen to Jiggy McCue. I needed to be certain there wasn't some small print that would force me to personally clean every toilet in town for life or something.

'I can wish for any three things I like?'

'Anything.'

'And you'll make them come true?'

'That's what it says in my job description.'

'So I could even wish for good luck if I wanted?'

'You could.'

'And get it?'

'In spades. But I'm required to give you this warning. Watch what you wish for. From this moment on, if you wish for something in my presence I have to deliver, and things can only be

34

changed back by a second wish. Think very carefully before you say the word "wish" – right?'

'Right. But just so I'm absolutely sure…if I said, for instance, "I wish you'd carry my kennel home for me, I wish I wasn't all covered in pee, and I wish my mother wouldn't keep pestering me to do my homework," you'd just wave your hand and it would be done?'

The fancy high-backed chair and footstool vanished. The genie fell with a bump to the ground.

'That has to be an all-time record,' he said.

'What does?'

He got up, shaking his head with amazement. Then he hoisted my kennel on his shoulders and set off in the direction of the Brook Farm Estate.

'You just blew your three wishes in a single sentence.'

'No, no,' I said, catching him up. 'They were just examples. I was just asking a question to clear things up.'

'I warned you. I was very clear about it. And what do you do in the very next breath? You say, "I wish you'd carry my kennel home for me, I wish I wasn't all covered in pee, and I wish my mother

wouldn't keep pestering me to do my homework."
You said "I wish" each time, so I have no choice but
to make these things happen.'

My knees shook. 'You mean that's it? I've had my
three wishes?'

'Am I not carrying your kennel?' he said.

'Yes, but...'

'And are you still covered in pee?'

I felt my clothes and hair. Bone dry, no scum, no
smell.

'No, but...'

'And won't your mother cease to pester you to do
your homework?'

'I don't know, will she?'

'She will.'

'And that really is all my wishes gone?'

'Yep. Your wish entitlement has been used up.
You are now absolutely wishless. Wishes that come
true are off your menu.'

There was quite a trudge in my step as we
walked home. At the house, I led the way round
the back. The genie followed me into the garden
and set the kennel down near Mum's rockery.

'So what now?' I asked, shoving a miserable

finger up the garden gnome's rear end.*

'I vanish in a puff of smoke and go back where you found me for another eternity. Thanks a lot, O Master.'

'Sorry.'

'Not half as sorry as I am. You think I *like* it down there?'

There was a puff of smoke and he was gone. I turned sadly away. I was about to put my key in the lock when the door sprang back.

'You're late!' my mother cried. 'Where have you been since school finished?'

'I had to bring my Woodwork project home.' I pointed it out to her. She stared at it blankly. 'It's a kennel,' I informed her.

'But we haven't got a dog,' she said.

'It's a PROJECT!' I yelled.

She jumped. 'Well there's no need to snap my head off.'

I took a deep calming breath. 'Er, Mum...'

'What?'

'I'm never going to do any homework again. Like *ever*. Homework and me will never cross paths from this day forth. What do you to say to that?'

---

* The secret place we keep the back-door key.

'Your homework,' she said. 'Nothing to do with me.'

Oh, he'd been a genie all right. And I really had used up the three wishes that could have turned my life around. Now how's *that* for bad luck?

Chapter Four

Angie Mint and Pete Garrett and I call ourselves the Three Musketeers. This isn't because we're really cool with swords and stuff, it's just that there's three of us. But we have a battle-cry: 'One for all and all for lunch'. You can't call yourselves the Three Musketeers, or even the One Musketeer, without a battle-cry. Pete and his dad and Angie and her mum all live under the same roof across the road from me, but they're not related. Well Angie and her mum are related and Pete and his dad are, but that's about it. I hadn't told P and A what happened the day before – the freak weather, the purple smoke from the dead chimney, me running home with a boy's best friend on public exhibition – but I couldn't keep the genie to myself. I phoned after tea and told them I was calling an urgent meeting of the Musketeers. The meeting was held in Angie's room because it's the only one with clean air. The three of us sat cross-legged on the floor

39

facing one another as I trotted out the essentials.

'You met a genie,' Pete said in a flat sort of voice when he'd heard all I wanted to tell him.

'I know, I know, you think I've cracked or I'm making it up. I don't blame you. I'd think the same if you told me something like this.'

'You have to admit it's a bit far-fetched,' Angie said.

'My entire recent life is far-fetched,' I reminded her.

'So where's this genie now?' Pete asked.

'He carried my kennel home, then vanished in a puff of smoke.'

'Why did he carry your kennel home?'

'Because I wished that he would.'

'That's all you had to do – wish and he'd do it?'

'Yes. Up to three times anyway.'

'So this genie gave you three wishes, and you used one of them to wish he'd carry your kennel home?'

I stared at the carpet between us in shame. 'Yes.'

Pete got up and walked slowly round me several times. Every now and then he bent down and pretended to inspect me like I'd just got off the saucer from Venus. I sighed. Standard Pete Garrett put-down. Angie didn't say a word, just looked at her fingernails.

'Nope,' Pete said after a while. 'Can't see any difference.'

'Difference?'

'Between the old McCue and the new improved version that you would naturally have asked for with one of the other wishes.'

'I didn't wish for anything like that.'

'No? What then? You wished for a big shiny castle on a hill? You wished for a secret cave stuffed with gold and jewels? You wished to be chief honcho of the Ranting Lane Board of Governors so you could close the dump down?'

'No, nothing like that.'

'So...what?'

I told them about the other two accidental wishes. Pete groaned. Angie still didn't speak or look at me.

'Well I was caught on the hop,' I said. 'It's not every day I get a genie bearing wishes.'

'You didn't get one this time,' Pete said.

'Eh?'

'You don't seriously expect us to swallow this drivel, do you?'

'You don't believe me?'

'Believe you met a genie? Get outta here!'

'So why ask me about my three accidental wishes?'

He came over all smug. 'Because I know you. Because if there were such things as genies, and if you were given three wishes, that's just the sort of naff stuff you would wish for.'

I glared at Angie, still inspecting her nails.

'Well? No comment from you? Nothing to say about my imaginary genie?'

She looked up at last. 'No, not right now.'

I trundled to my feet and swept to the door.

'All we've been through together, all the unbelievable things that have happened to us, and you still think I'm spinning a line when I tell you about something weird. One for all and all for lunch – that's a laugh!'

Pete yelled something after me as I went down the stairs, something stupid about genies, but I closed my ears. Couldn't shut his laughter out though. Didn't hear a peep out of Angie, but I reckoned she was probably laughing silently.

Mum was watching TV when I got in. Her favourite soap. I was about to go up to my room when the closing credits came on. I stopped. I still needed to spread the word about the genie and I was kind of short of eager listeners. I leaned in the door.

'Mum?'

She waved the remote in the air and turned the volume down. Not off, you notice. I'm not important enough to lose the theme of a four-nights-a-rotten-week soap.

'Yes, dear?'

'Mum, do you believe in genies?'

'I've nothing against them. I've a pair myself.'

'You've got a pair your...? You have a pair of *genies*?'

She half turned on the couch. 'Oh, don't tell me you've got through your new ones *already*. Jiggy, you've only had them since—'

I gripped the door handle. '*Genies*, mother, not *jeans*! You never should have had your ears pierced, you know.'

I hauled myself upstairs. Dad was on the

landing staring at the unlit ceiling light. I asked him why.

'Bulb's dead.'

'You're not thinking of changing it, are you?'

That would be a first. My father never changes light bulbs. Terrified of electricity. Electrical storms send him flying under the stairs with Stallone, our cat, and he hates Stallone.

'No chance,' he said. 'Twist the bulb too far and six million volts later I'm in a plastic urn on the mantelpiece. I'll get your mum to do it.'

'Dad, what would you say if I said I'd met a genie?'

He gave this some thought, then nodded sadly. 'Well, had to happen sometime. I'm sure she's very nice, Jig. Good luck, mate, you'll need it.'

I sighed. Parent World is in an alternative universe. I went to my room. In my room I went to the window and stood looking at the stars. The stars had been there since Christmas, so I started scraping them off with a fingernail. While I was scraping, my eyes strayed to my dogless kennel in the back garden below. It was still where the genie had put it, but Mum would move it first chance she got. My mother moves everything. It's a thing she has, tidying up and moving stuff, even when they don't need tidying and moving. I thought about the day. About probably being the only person for years who'd had his very own personal genie. I thought about the three wishes I could have asked for if my head had been screwed on instead of loosely attached with Velcro. I could have been really happy right now. Could have had my entire class queuing up to wait on me hand and foot. Better still, my teachers. I could have been living in luxury, surrounded by the latest high-tech digital whatnots, with parents who wanted to take me on holiday all the time and buy me stuff. I could have been taller, better looking, someone people listen to and think is brilliant. All right, I couldn't have got all this with just three wishes, but if I'd taken the time to work out the exact words I could probably have got several things in one go. And what had I done? Chucked everything away in a single breath. I would have given anything for another shot at those wishes. I'd even have given up the one that stopped my mother banging on about my lousy homework.

Hey. What?

I stopped scraping stars and looked hard at the kennel down below. There was a faint glow in the doggy doorway. A second after I noticed it, the glow dimmed to nothing. Maybe the kennel was glowing because it had been touched by the magical hands of a genie, I thought. Some sort of afterglow. Lucky kennel. No afterglow for me. My one chance of a better life was history.

That night I had a terrible nightmare. Not about the kennel, not about the genie, not even about making a pig's ear of the three wishes. I was down on my knees with my neck on this wooden block, and there was this creaking sound up above. I twisted my head to take a dekko. High up between two tall columns was this colossal blade. Suddenly there was a shout, like a signal, and – whooosh! – the blade came rattling down. I tried to pull my head out of the way, but it wouldn't budge. There was this horrible thud and everything went dark. Seconds passed. Then I opened my eyes, still in the dream, and I was looking up at the sky, which seemed to be moving because my head was rolling about on the ground. And I had an audience. An audience of enormous maggots. I was surrounded by them. There were hundreds of them, thousands, and they were laughing. Laughing at me, Jiggy McJerk, biggest joke around.

Chapter Five

Next morning, dull and early, I headed for school alone. Didn't want to talk to Pete and Angie after their vote of no confidence last night. But they caught me up before I reached the end of the street. Pete didn't waste a moment.

'Anything appeared in a puff of smoke recently, Jig?'

'Shut up.'

'I've been thinking about what you told us,' Angie said.

'So *now* you want to make the smart remark?' I said.

'You were serious, weren't you?'

'Serious? 'Bout what?'

'The Piddle Pool Genie.'

'The Piddle Pool Genie was a joke, Ange. I was pulling your leg.'

Best way I could think of to get the subject dropped.

'You were?' She sounded disappointed.

I managed a smirk. 'Sure fell for that one, didn't you?'

'Just *her* leg?' said Pete.

'What?' I said.

'You said you were pulling her leg. Just her leg or mine too?'

'Both.'

'Left or right?'

'Take your stupid pick.'

'Not all four?'

I hit him with my school bag.

'Save the gratuitous violence for the sports field, McCue!' bellowed a voice just behind us.

It was Mr Rice, our PE teacher, in his insane red tracksuit, jogging to school with Miss Weeks, our Deputy Head, in her nice green one.

'Morning, Angie,' said Miss W as they passed. 'Morning, Pete. Morning, Jiggy.'

'Morning, Miss,' we piped. Miss Weeks is OK, just has this dodgy taste in jogging partners.

We watched them jog to the kerb, then jog on the spot till the lights changed and the traffic stopped, then jog across. But a funny thing happened when they were about halfway. Mr Rice dropped to the ground suddenly and started doing press-ups. Yes, really! A couple of car drivers hooted, because it seemed like a terrific joke for a moment.

'I never knew Rice had a sense of humour,' said Pete.

'Brain's turned to mush,' I said. 'Happens to all PE teachers in the end.'

Miss Weeks had jogged on when Rice dropped, but she noticed he wasn't with her before she made it to the other side. She looked back, and when she saw what he was doing she also dropped to the ground. Not to do press-ups though. To do body crunches.

'This is not a way for teachers to behave in public,' Angie said loudly as we walked past them.

The lights changed as we reached the opposite curb. We looked round, expecting Ranting Lane's suddenly sporty kidders to leap to their feet and jog after us. But no. They stayed put, pressing up and crunching – faster. The traffic that could get round them went on its way, but the drivers who were forced to stay put started thumping their horns. Heads jerked out of windows shouting unkind suggestions as to what our PE teacher and Deputy Head could do with their press-ups and crunches. Crowds started to form on both pavements. Some laughed, some jeered, and all the time Mr Rice and Miss Weeks went faster and faster, like they'd been speeded up or something.

The lights changed again, and Rice and Weeks stopped exercising as suddenly as they'd started. They got up, looking dazed and embarrassed. Rice blushed the colour of his tracksuit. They headed for the curb. As they slipped into the crowd, hands over faces to thwart stray paparazzi, someone said: 'Hey, what's with him?'

Whoever said it wasn't talking about Mr Rice, but about a man in a business suit who was doing cartwheels along the pavement.

'Must be something in the water round here,' Angie said.

'Water?' I said – and suddenly I had it. Some of it anyway.

'Wo-ho!' said Pete, throwing his school bag in the air and flipping over on to his palms.

'Pete?' Angie and I said together.

But he was off, cartwheeling to school. Others flipped over on to their hands and cartwheeled along the pavement and across the road between vehicles. Non-cartwheelers gasped, chortled, whistled. A few looked worried, obviously fearing that the urge to cartwheel might take them next.

'This is not normal,' Angie said, slinging Pete's bag over her shoulder.

'You think?' I said.

And then I saw him. The character behind all this. He was wearing blue pyjamas and juggling with live kittens and puppy dogs, so it was kind of hard to miss him. People were ignoring him though. We get a lot of wacky street entertainers in our town. Most passers-by pretend they don't see or hear them so they won't have to drop a coin in their hat.

'This is all down to you, isn't it?' I said, marching up to him.

'I hope so,' he said, juggling.

'But what are you doing it for?'

'Just seeing if I've still got it after all this time.'

'Well now that you know you have, stop it. Put

everyone back on their feet – now.'

I was annoyed. I don't know why. Maybe I felt responsible, seeing as it was my thousand-and-first pee that had called him up.

'You can't give me orders,' the genie said. 'You're no longer my master.'

The juggled kittens and puppies started yapping and hissing at me as they flew up in the air and down again.

I leaned back, out of range. 'OK, scrub the order. Will you stop if I say please?'

'Please is good. Almost a magic word, please.'

The kittens and puppies disappeared. People stopped cartwheeling and started looking for things that had fallen out of their pockets.

'Who is this?' Angie asked, coming up behind me.

'One guess.'

'Not your genie?' I nodded. 'But you said...'

'It was easier. I thought you were going back to the Piddle Pool,' I said to the genie.

'Couldn't face it,' he said. 'The only thing I was looking forward to about having to serve a human again was a break from that hole. And what do you do? Ruin everything, in seconds.'

'I apologised for that.'

'Apologies change nothing.'

'I wouldn't want to go back there either,' Angie said. 'I mean, the Piddle Pool, not exactly the home of anyone's dreams.'

The genie's purple eyes took her in like she'd just crawled from under a rock.

'Is this…*anyone?*'

'Angie Mint,' I said. 'Friend. Listen, if you're sticking around for a while you have to stop making people do weird stuff. This is a very ordinary town full of very ordinary boring people. Mostly. They can't handle things like—'

The genie growled. He growled because he'd just turned into an eight foot tall purple-eyed grizzly bear. Angie and I jumped back like we were joined at the hip.

'Do you have to do things like that?' I said.

He laughed a deep growly laugh, then swapped the grizzly bod for normal size and a suit of armour with the visor down. Almost at once we heard a sound like someone banging coconuts together behind us. We stepped aside just in time to stop ourselves becoming hoof prints as a horse galloped by. The genie must have summoned the horse because he leapt on to its back and charged off down the street like a knight of old going into battle. Angie and I looked at one another. I knew from her expression that she was thinking the same as me. That this character might be more than just a genie. That he might be a genie who was so far out of his mind that he'd lost the address.

Chapter Six

We caught up with Pete just before registration. 'Done any good cartwheels recently?' I said. Revenge is sweet. Or should be. Wasted on Pete. He shook his head in amazement.

'Dunno what came over me. One minute I'm standing there with you two, the next...I didn't even know I could *do* cartwheels!'

We didn't tell him who'd made him do them, wasn't time, so for the first half of the morning it was our secret, Angie's and mine. We made the most of it, really milked it, and by morning break Pete was crazy to know why we kept glancing at one another and rolling our eyes. So we took him aside and told him. And he still didn't believe a word.

He started to believe after break, though, in Science.

Our Science teacher, Mr Flowerdew, was a serious man. Very tall and pale and unwell-looking. He never laughed, hardly ever smiled, and always wore a black suit. The only thing that brightened him up was the flower in his lapel. He wore a fresh flower every day. He also wore dark glasses all the time, like someone with really sensitive eyes. In the shades and suit, with that pale serious face, he looked like a Mafia hitman. But he didn't tell us off much, and he wasn't too strict, so we didn't mind him too much.

The Science lab is on the top floor. Obvious why. If something explodes it won't disrupt the lesson above. It's a big high room, with windows all along both sides, and it gets pretty steamy there in summer. It was summer now. We would have opened the windows to let some air in, but interior decorators had painted them shut three terms ago and no one had bothered to fix them. Everyone had their jackets off except Mr Flowerdew. I was just wondering what kept him from passing out when he swayed suddenly, went even paler than usual, and little beads of sweat appeared on his forehead.

'You all right, sir?' several voices said at once.

He mumbled something and tottered out of the room. No one tottered after him. We know our place. Kids are expected to stay put during earthquakes, hurricanes, volcanic eruptions and killer bee invasions unless there's been a Special Drill to tell us to file out quietly.

It was about then that something happened to the twenty-three trillion iron filings we'd been pointlessly dragging round bits of glass with magnets. They jumped off all the bits of glass, zoomed across the room, and didn't stop until they hit something.

An invisible face.

An invisible face that was no longer invisible.

With iron filings clinging to it, every pore, hair, lip and eyelid showed as clearly as if a can of spray paint had blasted it.

'It's him,' Angie mouthed at me.

'Never've guessed,' I mouthed back.

I was half off my stool, all set to race over and fling myself in front of the hovering face to give it a chance to disappear in private. But I didn't need to. The face shook suddenly like a cat with fleas and the iron filings fell to the floor. I rushed over anyway. 'You still there?' I whispered, prodding nothing. He obviously wasn't. The class was pretty

58

spooked. They gathered round the heap of iron filings on the floor as if expecting them to rise up as a face again. Pete pulled Angie and me to one side.

'You know anything about that?'

'Might,' I said.

'Tell me.'

'Tried to tell you earlier, and last night, you didn't believe it.'

'You mean the stupid genie stuff?' I zipped my lips. 'Does he mean the stupid genie stuff?' he said to Angie.

'Might,' she said.

'Come on, talk to me, what's it all about, what's going on?'

I sighed, then ticked off the bare bones of the story so far.

'Piddle Pool. Genie. Street. Press-ups, crunches, cartwheels. School. Science lab. Iron filings. Face. Scab.'

'Scab?'

'You. For not believing me.'

Just then the lunch bell went, and with no teacher to tell us not to rush we stampeded out of the room and down the stairs, yelling all the way. Mr Flowerdew was already outside, gulping playground air. He looked a bit better than before, but not a lot. I was about to ask him if he was OK when Mr Dent came out of the Woodwork shop and told him he looked rough. Mr Flowerdew thanked him and said he thought he might find a quiet spot to sit down for a while. Then he wandered off to the Concrete Garden, which was annoying because that's where we go to eat our lunch most days. Couldn't go there with a teacher there.

Mr Dent was on playground duty today. When some teachers are on PD you don't like to raise your voice or move too fast or they threaten to tear your fingernails out one by one, but when Mr Dent's on things are pretty relaxed. Pete and Angie and I strolled round the edge of the playground, away from everyone else. This was because now that Pete knew the genie wasn't a figleaf of my imagination he wanted all the details again, in longhand.

'So this genie comes out of the Piddle Pool, right?'

'Right.'

'Why to you? I mean why you?'

I still hadn't mentioned the lifetime of secret tinkles, and wasn't going to. A person can handle just so much humiliation in one week. I shrugged.

'Guess I just happened to be in the vicinity when he felt like stretching his legs.'

'And he really gave you three wishes?'

'Yes.'

'And instead of wishing to be rich, handsome and a really interesting person...?'

'Yes.'

We passed the Concrete Garden, where Mr Flowerdew was sitting feebly, and came to Rubbish Bin Corner. This isn't really a corner, it's a sort of alcove where they keep the big black bins they put the school dinners in. It's also where a lot of kids go for a sly smoke, but there were none there today when I glanced in. Someone else was though.

'Whoa,' I said.

Pete and Angie whoaed. Crouching behind one of the bins was a dreadlocked teenager in green wellies, embarrassing white ballet tights, and a string vest.

'Who is *he*?' Pete said.

'Don't you recognise him without the iron filings?' I said.

'That's *him*? That's your *genie*?'

'Yup.'

'Isn't he a bit young?'

'He's older than he looks.'

'Also a bit underdressed?'

'I don't think he's got the hang of modern fashions yet.' I went into the alcove. 'What are you doing here?' I said to the cowering genie.

'Hiding.'

He looked really edgy. His dreadlocks were all quivery, twisting round one another like long nervous fingers.

'Who from?' Angie asked.

'The genie,' he said.

'The genie? But you're the genie.'

'The other one, I'm hiding from the *other* genie. I'd hardly be hiding from myself, would I?'

'You might if you looked in a mirror,' said Pete.

The skulking genie scowled. 'Who's this?'

'Another friend,' I said. 'Sometimes. Did you mean what you just said? There's a second genie?'

'There is. I didn't know it till I came here. And if

he sees me, if he touches me...'

He shuddered horribly.

'Where is he then?'

'Out there.'

He pointed at the playground but kept well back so's not to be seen. We looked out. Boys were yelling, charging about, thumping one another. Girls were skipping like little angels on long ropes or standing in groups talking about hair. Mr Dent stood with his hands in his pockets, smiling like playground duty was the highlight of his day. That was it.

'I see no genie,' said Pete.

'Just kids,' I said.

'No adult?' the genie said hopefully.

'Only our Woodwork teacher, Mr Dent,' Angie said.

The hope drained out of the purple eyes.

'Mr Dent? Woodwork teacher? Whatever he calls himself, whatever he pretends to be, he's a genie. And he's dangerous. To me personally.'

It was hard to keep the laughter in, thinking of our friendly Woodwork teacher as a genie, but I frowned at the others so they'd give it a go.

'What makes you think Mr Dent's a genie?' Angie asked.

My ex-genie tapped his head.

'Takes one to know one?' Pete said.

'What do you mean dangerous?' I said. 'Dangerous how?'

'That's for me to know and you not to.'

He seemed keen to drop the subject, so I asked him why he was hanging round school. He told us that he'd never been in a school before. Just popped in to see what it was like here.

'Invisibly?' Angie said.

'I didn't want to be seen.'

'Very wise, dressed like that,' said Pete.

'You were seen,' I reminded him.

'I hadn't expected iron filings.'

'Why did they fly to you anyway?'

'Must be my magnetic personality.'

'Do you have a name?' This was Angie.

He came over all suspicious. 'Why do you want to know?'

'Just curious.'

'Well, I don't suppose it matters,' he said. 'Call me JR.'

'That's not a name,' said Pete, 'it's just a couple of letters.'

The genie glared at him. 'It's the initials of my chosen name.'

'Which is?'

'Which is appropriate to the place I come from.'

'I hear the place you come from is a pool of pee,' said Pete.

'I don't think I like your friend,' the genie said to me.

'You wouldn't be the first,' I answered.

'What *does* JR stand for?' Angie asked.

'Take a guess,' he said. 'Take three.'

'How about three wishes instead?' Pete said.

'I'm out of wishes.' He glanced at me. 'Ask my ex-master here.'

'Jimmy Riddle,' I said.

His eyebrows shot up into his dreadlocks. 'What?'

'Your name. Jimmy Riddle. Am I right?'

'Yes. But how…?'

'Rhyming slang. We widdle, we piddle, your name's Jimmy Riddle.'

'You're smarter than you look,' he said.

'Thanks.'

'Riddle,' said Pete. 'Does that mean you *do* riddles?'

JR narrowed his eyes at him. 'Are you making fun of my name?'

'No, I'm not making fun of your stupid name, I'm asking a question, do you do riddles, yes or no?'

'I'm a genie, I can do anything.'

'So let's hear some.'

'I'm more inclined to turn you into a toad,' JR said.

'Oh, don't do that,' I said. 'Pete's already quite a way down the food chain.'

'Can't you ask him a riddle just to shut him up?' Angie said.

JR gave a bored sigh. 'You humans, such small minds. But...' He drew himself up, and, certain that Pete would be no match for him, said: 'What is too much for one, enough for two, but nothing for three?'

'A secret,' said Pete, right off.

JR rocked like a skittle. Angie and I grinned at one another. Pete knows more rotten jokes than I've had bad haircuts.

Our genie friend took another shot. 'What question can you never honestly answer "yes" to?'

'"Are you asleep?"' Pete said.

There was a sound like grinding teeth. JR didn't seem to like being outsmarted.

'How can you tell two identical trees apart?' he demanded.

'Dunno about you,' said Pete, 'but I listen to their barks.'

Steam shot from JR's ears. 'What goes around the world, yet stays in a corner?'

'A postage stamp. Hey, is this the best you can do? I've seen better riddles on gravestones.'

'Five people at a picnic, five apples in a basket,' JR said with a snarl. 'Everyone takes an apple but one remains in the basket. How can this be?'

'The last person took the basket, with the last apple still in it,' said Pete.

'I *really* don't like you,' JR said.

'Sorry to hear that, I'm a big fan of yours.'

'Mr Dent's coming!' said Angie, pulling back from the corner where she'd been keeping watch.

JR's hands shook. 'H-him?'

'Yes. Mr Dent the Woodwork genie.'

'I'm off.'

'Oh, must you?' said Pete.

JR disappeared in a puff of angry smoke seconds before Mr Dent looked round the corner and found us whistling tunelessly by the bins.

'Listen,' he said, 'I don't want to cramp your style, but if you don't give up you'll regret it when you're older.'

'No, no,' I protested, waving JR's smoke away, 'you've got it all wrong…'

Mr Dent smiled. 'Can't fool me, son, I've been there.'

He looked at our feet. We were standing on an incriminating carpet of dog-ends.

Chapter Seven

We didn't see JR for the rest of the school day, but knowing he could pop up any time – could even be lurking invisibly nearby – didn't help me relax. I like to relax in class. I also wanted to talk to Pete and Angie about him, but teachers aren't too keen on people talking in lessons. It's not fair. They do, all the time.

As we beetled out of the gates at the end of the afternoon we crashed into Neil Downey, guillotine maker, maggot mangler. We stepped smartly back. Nobody likes to get too near Downey. He has this smell, like very old meat.

'Don't forget my party,' he grinned.

'What party?' said Pete.

'My birthday party, tomorrow night.'

'Why do we have to remember your birthday party?'

'Because you're coming,' Downey said.

'I don't think so,' said Pete.

'Think again,' said Angie. 'I accepted on your behalf.'

'On both our behalves,' I muttered quietly.

'Well you can just unaccept on *my* behalf,' Pete said.

Angie gripped his arm and gave him a Very Heavy look.

'You're going. We all are. We're really looking *forward* to it.'

'Oh,' said Pete, or it might have been 'Ow'. Didn't matter which because he knew he was going to Downey's party. Angie had spoken and you don't go against the Mint if you want your legs to keep bending the comfortable way. Didn't stop him arguing though.

'Hang on,' he said to Downey. 'Your birthday was the other week. I remember Miss Weeks telling everyone, like she thought we'd be interested.'

'I didn't have a party then,' Downey said. 'My dad was busy with his new stock.' He leaned forward. 'There's going to be *entertainment*.'

We leaned back, holding our breath. 'Entertainment?'

'Yeah! It's gonna be *great*!'

And he skipped off, alone. We breathed again.

'What was that about his dad's new stock?' I asked.

'Isn't his old fella some sort of farmer?' Angie said.

'Don't know, don't care.'

'Some mates you are,' said Pete. 'I would never accept an invitation to a Downey party. I can't even bear to be near him.'

'Who can?' said Angie. 'Don't worry, we'll get out of it at the last minute. Say our parents are playing up or something.'

'You mean we're not actually going?'

'Get real, Garrett. Can you really see me playing Pass-the-Parcel with Dungheap Downey?'

'So why say we're going in the first place?'

'He was trotting round inviting everyone in sight, and you couldn't see daylight for excuses, so when he got to me I accepted, to cheer him up.'

'He might not be so cheerful when we don't arrive,' I pointed out.

'His problem,' said Ange.

We set off, dragging our school bags. It was a

71

nice day. Too nice to rush home, so we stopped off at the Councillor Snit Memorial Park. It was pretty peaceful there. Just half a dozen teenage girls dropping ciggy ash into their prams, the odd dog sniffing the droppings of other odd dogs, a few overturned benches, bushes decorated with crisp packets, a big blue tent by the boating lake.

'Wonder what that is?' Angie said.

'It's a tent, Ange,' I explained patiently.

'Let's take a look.'

When we got to the tent we saw a notice tacked to a tree.

> STARVING
> ARTISTS
> SALE

'Who'd want to buy a starving artist?' Pete said.

'Not many going by the crowds,' I said.

If there'd been someone sitting by the entrance flaps taking money we wouldn't have bothered, but there wasn't, so we went in – and immediately regretted it. Inside, there were all these trestle tables covered with watercolours and oil paintings, with more on display boards behind. Everywhere you looked there were pictures of pretty landscapes, bowls of flowers, cross-eyed babies, cute little kittens. Sitting proudly on plastic chairs by their work were all these neatly dressed Golden Oldies, and they were smiling at us (the only visitors) like we'd come to buy something or something.

'They don't *look* starving,' Pete whispered.

'Don't look much like artists either,' I whispered back.

'Let's go.'

'Better look round now we're here,' Angie said.

'I have,' Pete said. 'And I've seen enough.'

He spun to leave. Angie grabbed him by the weedy little bicep, spun him back.

'We can't go yet. We're probably the only people they've seen all day. They'll be disappointed if we don't even *seem* interested.'

'You're going soft,' he said.

'And you're going in.'

She marched him to the first table and gripped the back of his neck so he had to look at the paintings on it. I tagged along because I didn't want her chasing after me and dragging me back by the hair.

We strolled as quickly as Angie would let us from table to table. All the way round the tent these non-starving, non-arty eyes followed us hopefully. Angie said nice things about the pictures and got thank-yous and happy smiles in return. Pete and I couldn't think of anything nice to say, so kept quiet.

There was only one person there who looked like he might be both starving and an artist. His pitch was the very last, just inside the exit flaps (which doubled as the entrance flaps). He was pretty ragged, needed a shave, looked like he should be standing outside Woolworths selling *Fat Chance*, the magazine for the homeless. His paintings were all sizes, from pretty small to quite big, and every one of them was crammed with wiggly little shapes. My stomach turned over.

'Those paintings,' I said with a suddenly dry mouth. 'Remind you of anything?'

'Neil Downey's maggots,' said Pete.

The only difference between Downey's maggots and the painted wigglies was that the painted wigglies didn't move and were all the colours of the rainbow. Enough like them to make me gag, though. I shot out of the tent.

Pete and Angie followed. Pete laughed and ran off, started kicking a squashed lager can around the park.

'You all right, Jig?' Angie asked.

'Never better,' I gasped, hoiking my stomach the right way up again.

'Why can't you take a picture of a man with a wooden leg?' Pete yelled.

We didn't answer.

'Because wooden legs don't have lenses! How far can a dog run into the woods?'

Angie and I strolled away from the tent.

'Halfway! Any further and he'd be running out!'

He booted the lager can up a tree and came after us. We were almost at the gates when two familiar faces came in, along with two familiar bodies. My mother and Janet Overton from next door.

'What are you three doing here?' Mum demanded.

'It's a public park, we're allowed,' I said. 'Why aren't you at work?'

'Half day off. Janet and I thought we'd take a

look at the Starving Artists exhibition.'

'We've just been,' said Angie.

'Anything there?' asked Janet O.

'No,' said Pete. 'They deserve to starve.'

Chapter Eight

Back on the estate Pete and Angie went to their house and I went to mine. Seemed best to do it that way. I shunted into the kitchen and heaved a two-litre bottle of Diet Cola to my lips. I'd taken three and a half gulps before I realised the stuff in the bottle wasn't much like the description on the label. The label shouldn't have read Diet Cola. It should have read Diet Piddle. I ran to the sink and spat like a madman. Then I stuck my trap under the tap and gulped water – until I noticed that the water was identical to the stuff in the bottle, except it had no bubbles. I smacked the tap and ran to the freezer, whipped out a lime ice-lolly, plunged it into the McCue gob. And...

It was no longer lime!

I threw the lolly at the sink and attacked the biscuit tin. I was about to fold a chocolate digestive into my mouth when I suddenly came over cautious and sank a nervous tooth or two into the edge. Relief. Pure plain chocolate digestive. I rammed the whole thing against my tonsils and hammered a couple more after it. My mouth was so full that I couldn't munch, but the flavour was what counted, and the flavour was good.

When I finally managed to get the chocky bics down, I stood gasping while the questions started throwing themselves at me.

Question 1: What's happening here?

Question 2: Why does everything liquid taste of widdle?

Yes, there were only two, but they were big ones, and I had no doubt that they shared an answer. I glared round. 'Where are you?' I shouted. 'I know you're here, come out where I can see you!'

'In here!' a voice called. Not JR's voice though. Dad's.

I went along the hall to the living room. He was sprawling in his favourite tatty armchair watching horse racing on TV and wearing a fireman's helmet. The hat wasn't a surprise, he collects wacky headgear, my dad. He'd obviously been to Help the Aged, his favourite clothes shop.

'First Mum, now you,' I said. 'Don't you people

do a full day's work any more?'

'Should this thing be silent?' he asked instead of answering.

He meant the TV. No sound was coming from it.

'Try the volume,' I said.

'Volume?'

'Oh, I get it.'

The remote was on top of the set and he didn't feel like stirring his sad old carcass. I marched over to the TV and turned the sound up. Dad sprang forward in his chair, staring at the screen with the expression of a two-year-old who just came across Tellytubbies for the first time. It was then that I noticed something about him. I moved closer, sure that it must be a trick of the light. I was almost in his lap when he looked up at me and smiled. His eyes were purple.

'Dad?' I said.

'Son?' As he said this, one of his front teeth sparkled like a toothpaste ad.

I rushed to the TV and hit the off button. Then I rushed back to the armchair and leaned over the creature in the fireman's helmet masquerading as my father.

'*What are you doing in my dad's body?!*' I yelled.

'It's not his body, it's just a very good copy.'

'Well lose it, it makes me uncomfortable.'

'Me too,' he said as he slimmed down to his usual shape and the fireman's helmet turned into dreadlocks.

'How did you get in?' I demanded.

'Your father's body?'

'The house.'

'Same way I get in anywhere, man. I materialised.'

'Well, materialise off, this is private property.'

'You're being very hostile,' he said.

'Yeah, well maybe it's something to do with coming home and finding that the cola, water and lollies have been turned to pee. Why did you *do* that?'

'I didn't do it. Liquids just change when I'm around. Don't worry, it'll change back once I go.'

'So go, go!'

'You were glad enough to see me when I had three wishes for you.'

'I'd be glad enough to see you now if you had three wishes for me, but you don't, so sling your hook.'

He put his hands behind his head and leaned back.

'I like it here, man.'

'What's all this "man" stuff all of a sudden?' I asked.

'Isn't that what teenagers say?'

'You're not a teenager, you just look like one.'

'I know, but it's weird. I'm getting this compulsion to say "man" all the time, walk with my knees out, chew gum, hang with the guys.'

'What guys?'

'You can't have everything.'

'Look, you can't stay here,' I said. 'There's no room for one thing, and for another my parents would probably notice an unscripted lodger.'

'Perhaps I'll find a little place of my own.'

'Good idea. I hear there are some terrific little places in Antarctica.'

The phone rang. I slapped the receiver to my ear. '*What!*'

'Jiggy, why are you shouting?' It was Mum.

'Vocal exercises. Is this a social call?'

'I just rang to ask you to put the kettle on, that's all.'

'Kettle?'

'And put some water in for a change. You and your

father seem to think the water appears by magic.'

'The water I know does. Why do you want me to put some in the kettle?'

'Because I'm gasping for a cup of tea.'

'Mother,' I said, 'you're not here. You're at the other end of this line. You can't pour tea down a phone line. Well, you could, but it probably wouldn't go far.'

'I'm on my way home. Put a saucer on the cup to keep it warm if I'm not back.'

'Why do you want a warm saucer?'

'You're in a very silly mood, Jiggy.'

'Keeps me sane,' I said, and hung up. I turned to JR. 'My mother's coming home and she wants a cup of tea. What do I do?'

'Don't ask me, I've never made tea.'

'No, I mean it won't actually *be* tea, will it?'

'Like I said, it'll wear off soon enough. I better make myself scarce if your mother's coming home. Mothers worry me.'

'Worry me, too,' I said. 'Specially when I have to give them a cup of pee.'

JR flicked a finger and disappeared. Five seconds later he reappeared.

'Forgot the puff, man.'

There was a puff of smoke. I flinched. When I unflinched he was gone again and there was a hole in the carpet. I grabbed Stallone, who was passing, and parked him on the hole.

'Now don't move, Stal. *Ever*. From now on this hole is your hole. Guard it with one of those nine lives.'

Stallone's whiskers quivered. 'Go fry your kneecaps,' he growled in Cat-ese, and strolled out with his tail up.

I considered packing my father's Help the Aged duffel bag and leaving home before Mum arrived. But leaving home isn't something you do lightly when the head of the house makes the best chips in the world, so I went to the kitchen, turned the cold tap on, and filled the kettle with urine. Maybe she wouldn't notice. My mother's always trying unusual teas. I could say that some free samples came through the door. Tell her it was Lapsang Peechong. Or Darpeeling.

She came in about ten minutes later. She was carrying something under her arm. It was wrapped in pink newspaper. The something, not the arm.

'Whassat?'

'I bought one of the Starving Artists' paintings.'

My heart plunged to my socks. My mother's taste is not predictable. Sometimes she gets it right, other times you can only slap your forehead in I-must-be-dreaming amazement. What was she going to lumber us with from that crummy exhibition? A bowl of flowers, a hay cart with the sun going down, a cute little kitten? I couldn't stand it if it was a cute little kitten. A cute little kitten staring at me every time I came down for breakfast would ruin my day, every day. I stiffened my upper lip and squared my manly shoulders.

'Show me.'

She tore the *Financial Times* off and held the Starving Artist pic up for me to see. It wasn't a cute little kitten. It wasn't a landscape or bowl of flowers. Wasn't even a drooling baby with its hair standing up like a brush. It was one of the pictures painted by the ragged unshaven man. One of the ones that reminded me of Downey's maggots.

'Unusual, isn't it?' Mum said as my stomach hit the ceiling. I didn't answer. Couldn't. She put the picture down. 'My tea brewed?'

I shot through to the kitchen. As if nightmares

about maggots weren't bad enough, I now had a picture to remind me of them. Wonderful. I took the warm saucer off the cup with a shaking hand. Splashed some milk in.

'Jiggy! What happened to the carpet?'

Ulp. I'd forgotten the hole in the carpet. I carried the tea to the living room where Mum was poking the hole with some toes.

'Stallone,' I said.

'Stallone?'

'He was lurking around here when I went out. Has to be him. I don't know why you don't just turn him into a wall hanging and be done with it.'

I left the cup of steaming pee within reach and headed for the door. I needed to be somewhere else. Somewhere I wouldn't be asked the kind of questions I couldn't answer without crossing my fingers in triplicate behind my back.

Chapter Nine

I rang Pete and Angie's doorbell. No one answered. I rang again. Same. And again. A window finally opened up above.

'Will you stop ringing that stupid bell?!' Pete yelled.

'I will if you come down and open the stupid door!' I yelled back.

'I'm on my computer!'

'And I'm on the step! Lemme in.'

I leaned on the bell to show I meant business.

'All right, all right, I'm coming, I'm coming!'

Seconds later I heard him thudding down the stairs.

'I'm doing this for you, you know!' he said, opening up.

'Well thanks, Pete. I'll open a door for you some time. Where's Angie?'

'Room.'

He thudded upstairs again and slammed his door.

I also went up, but not thudding and not to his room. I knocked on Angie's door, which was closed. Music was playing on the other side, which is probably why she didn't hear the bell. Or perhaps she heard but didn't feel like answering. That's Ange for you. She heard my knock though. Well, my third knock, which was pretty loud.

'Shove off.' Standard Angie greeting.

'It's Jig.'

'Password?'

'Haven't a clue.'

'OK.'*

I went in. She was reading a big fat book.

'Ange,' I said. 'That genie's going to be a problem.'

She turned the music down. 'Why, what's he done now?'

I told her about the contaminated liquids and the hole in the carpet.

'This could just be the beginning,' I said. 'We have to get shot of him before things get ugly. I'm calling in the Musketeers.'

'The Musketeers are already on it,' she said, and

---

* 'Haven't a clue' is the only password we can all remember.

held up her book. I read the title. *Genies: All There Is To Know.*

'Where'd you get that?'

'Found it in the bookcase. It says here that it's a translation from ancient texts by this professor type. How's about that then?'

'You find a book about genies on your bookcase right after we meet one for the first time?' I said. 'Doesn't that strike you as a bit of a coincidence?'

'They happen. It's probably one of Mum's. She used to read all sorts before we moved here and got cable. Some fascinating stuff here.' She turned back a page. 'Like, for instance, genies can change into anything they want—'

'I knew that.'

'But not only people and animals. Says here they can become insects, birds, flowers, trees, plus various non-living objects, like stones and runs.'

'Runs?'

'I think it's a misprint. Probably meant to be ruins.'

'Doesn't leave much they *can't* change into,' I said.

'Not a lot, no.'

'But genies are mythical beings, aren't they?

Half that stuff is probably made up.'

'The other half might not be. Like…"Genies take pleasure in punishing humans who do them harm. In wreaking punishment they can be very inventive." Better be careful how you handle him, just in case. I'd hate to see you wreaked.'

I sat down on the floor. There was a big soft bright cushion nearby. I put it between me and the wall. Comfy.

'New cushion?' I said.

She looked up from the book. 'Mum got it for me.' She screwed her face up. 'Have to go. Clashes with the curtains.'

'Yeah, my mum clashes with the curtains too.'

Just then Pete wandered in holding a sheet of A4.

'Waste of time,' he said.

'Life?' I said. 'Or something else?'

'He's been looking up genie info on the Net,' Angie said.

'Not like Pete to do something that's not for his benefit.'

'I told him to.'

'Oh.'

'Let's have what you've got,' she said to Pete.

89

'I typed the word "genie" to see what came up,' Pete said, 'thinking there'd be all sorts of guff on geezers in turbans with lamps and all, but the only ones like that were in ancient stories.'

'The *Arabian Nights*,' Angie said.

'How'd you know that?'

'Because I read,' she said. 'Books,' she added. 'The *Arabian Nights* is a collection of stories told over a thousand and one nights by this girl Scheherazade to this king who kept getting married, then executing his wives before the day was out.

'Cool,' said Pete.

'A thousand and one?' I said.

'Yeah, but old Sherry, she was a smart cookie,' Angie went on. 'She knew how to get the king's interest and keep her head. Night after night she told him a new story, and always kept the ending till morning so he'd want to hear what happened. Then she'd start another one.'

'I'd have executed her *for* telling me stories,' Pete said.

'That's because you're an illiterate peasant.' Angie said. 'The king was so impressed that she knew a thousand and one stories that he didn't kill her when she ran out of them. Far as I know they lived happily ever after. Till they died anyway.'

'Another coincidence,' I mused. 'Thousand and one nights, thousand and one pees.'

They gawped at me blankly and I remembered that I hadn't told them about my lifetime of secret visits to the Piddle Pool, or that it was the thousand-and-first that had brought JR up from the piddly deep. I told them now, had to, embarrassing as it was. Pete fell to the floor, doubled up.

'So it's your fault he's here,' Angie said. 'In that case you deserve to be wreaked.'

'Well, how was I to know what would happen? I just wanted some luck for a change.'

'Sometimes I can't believe *my* luck, stuck with you two.' She kicked Pete, still rolling around the floor, chortling. 'Get a grip, you.'

When he'd got the best grip he was capable of, she told him to read the stuff he'd found on the Internet.

'What I came up with,' he said, 'apart from *Arabian Nights* rubbish, is...' He read from his sheet, while lying on Angie's imitation sheepskin rug.

'Genie Genetic Engineering (cloning), Genie Garage Door Openers (handles and hinges), Domestic Genie (vacuum cleaners), The Reading Genie (a little deckchair you lean your stupid book against), Genie Particle and Gas Filters (whatever they are), Genie Travel (travel agent), and Lawn Genie (motor mower). The rest are genie-type games. Lots of those. Might download some.'

He tossed the sheet of paper aside, flipped over on the imitation sheepskin rug and started plucking imitation wool.

'Hey look,' I said. 'A little bird.'

It was sitting on the window ledge, all perky, looking in the open window.

'Sweet,' said Ange.

'Good with chips,' said Pete.

'Perhaps it's hungry,' I said.

'Well it's come to the wrong place,' Angie said. 'I don't keep bird food in my bedroom.' She was more interested in the genie book spread across her knees. 'This one could be useful. "Ways to get rid of troublesome genies".'

I leant over her and she showed me. 'Hey,' I said.

'Shall I read it out?' she asked.

'Yes. No, wait.'

I'd remembered that JR could be invisible when he felt like it. He might have followed me over the road and be squatting invisibly on the ceiling hanging on our every word. I cupped my hand round Angie's nearest ear. She pulled away.

'What are you doing?' she said.

'Want to tell you something.'

'So tell me.'

I winked meaningfully at her and jerked my head at the ceiling where JR might be squatting invisibly.

'Jig, have you lost it?'

'Ange,' I said, winking hard. 'Pay attention. I'm trying to be *secretive* here.'

'SECRETIVE?' Pete roared from the imitation sheep on the floor. 'WHAT'S THE BIG SECRET, JIG?'

I sighed. 'Never mind.'

'No, tell us,' said Angie.

'I was trying to. On the quiet.' I winked again. 'In case we're not *alone*.'

She still looked puzzled for a mo, but then her frown cleared.

'Oh. Got you.'

She leaned closer for me to cup her ear. I cupped.

'In a few days the Piddle Pool will become part of the leisure centre car park,' I whispered. 'If this book tells us how to send JR back there before they fill it in, he could be down there *for ever*.'

I decupped. Angie, all bright-eyed, cupped my ear.

'Better keep quiet about the car park. He might not know, and if we mention that the Piddle Pool's going to be tarmacked he might never go back.'

I recupped. 'What do you think I'm doing this for? You think whispering in cupped ears is my way of broadcasting news to the entire civilised *world*?'

'Good thinking,' she said, not bothering to cup.

'What's going on?' Pete demanded.

'Nothing,' said Angie.

'So why all the cupping and whispering?'

'Tell you later.'

'Hey, the little birdy's coming in,' I said.

It had hopped over the ledge and now stood on top of Angie's chest of drawers, glancing about like it was trying to decide whether to move in or not.

Pete sat up. 'Got something I can hit it with, Ange?'

'Don't you dare,' she said.

94

'I just want to stun it, not kill it. When it's unconscious we can drop it back outside where it belongs.'

'Where Stallone or some other neighbourhood villain will get it,' I said.

'Leave it,' said Angie. 'So long as it doesn't do its business on my pillow it can stick around for a while.'

'You two are no fun,' Pete said, and went back to plucking the imitation sheepskin.

'Tell us how to get rid of troublesome genies,' I said to Angie.

'What about...?' She winked meaningfully.

'This is different. It's just a book, nothing heavy.'

She read out the first way to get rid of troublesome genies.

'Poach three frogs in milk and pluck their eyes out. Drop the eyes into a tankard of warm beer. In three days your genie will have gone blind and as weak as a poached frog, and will probably move to another neighbourhood.'

'Probably move,' I said. 'No guarantee. Could still be a pest.'

Angie read the second way to get rid of troublesome genies.

'Roll up a friend in a rug and carry him to open

land. Place a stuffed owl on the rolled rug with the friend still inside, and say the words, "Jinn, ghul, ifrit or n'erk, begone from here, you lousy jerk." '

'This is a modern translation, right?' I said.

'Leave rug, friend and stuffed owl overnight. In the morning the owl will have flown – and so will the genie.'

'What about the friend?' Pete said.

'Only one way to find out,' I said.

I started towards him, hands like claws. He leapt off the sheepless rug and relocated to Angie's rocking chair with his knees drawn up to his chest. The sudden movement startled the little bird, which flapped around the room a few times before landing on Angie's bookshelf. It was then that I noticed something I hadn't noticed before.

The bird had purple eyes.

'Find the genie's home base,' Angie said, reading method three. *'If it's a lamp, block the spout with beeswax. If a bottle—'*

'Ange,' I said nervously.

'Quiet,' she snapped. *'If a bottle, replace the stopper, cork or cap with soft soap. If the genie's base is liquid, encircle it with—'*

'Angie, there's something you ought to know…'

'Will you shut up? I'm reading. *If the genie's base is liquid, encircle it with fire and throw a piece of fresh cod into it. In twenty-four hours the homeless genie will have moved on.*'

'This professor type is yanking our chains,' said rocking Pete.

'I was starting to think the same thawk!' Angie said, and threw *Genies: All There Is To Know* in the air.

She said 'thawk' and chucked the book because the little bird on the bookshelf had suddenly grown a lot bigger, changed shape, lost the feathers and beak, and sprouted dreadlocks. Purple ones.

'Good book?' said JR, catching it as it came down.

He'd gone the whole teen hog this time. His idea of it anyway. He wore jeans with the knees ripped out, black leather waistcoat with silver studs, no shirt. His bare arms were covered in tattoos, a silver cross on a thin chain was attached to his chin, and his head was shaved to about six centimetres above his ears. The purple dreads stood up on top like a little bed of Martian flowers.

'That's what I was trying to tell you,' I said to Angie.

'Well, next time try harder. I nearly had a stroke.'

'I knew there was something about that bird,' said Pete.

'No you didn't,' I said. 'You just like to bash things.'

'Should have let me. Heard any bad riddles lately, Genius?' he said to JR.

JR ignored him, just turned some pages of the book.

'How is it,' I said, 'that if you can change into anything you like – birds, bears, knights, fathers – you always come back to that body?'

'I get cool vibes with it, man,' he said, still flipping through the book. 'I dig the buzz, the heat, the wallop. Hey, wasn't this the bit you were so taken with – "Ways to get rid of troublesome genies"?'

'We were only looking,' Angie said.

'Course you were.'

'Didn't take it seriously,' I said.

'Course you didn't.' He handed the book back to

Angie. 'You're far too cool to believe everything you read, yeah?'

'Specially if it's written by a genie expert,' said Pete.

'Genie expert?' JR said. 'What's the cat's name?'

'What's Stallone got to do with anything?' I said.

'I mean the genie expert, dude.'

'He's called...' Angie looked at the author's name on the cover. 'Professor P P Eineg.'

JR stroked the chain hanging from his chin and gazed thoughtfully over our heads.

'I wonder what the P P stands for?'

'Could be anything,' I said. 'Paul, Peter, Patrick...'

'Petronella, Poppy, Phyllis,' said Angie.

'Plonker, Prat, Pee-Brain,' said Pete.

'Or Piddle,' said JR. 'Pool, even.'

Angie and I had a good laugh at that. Things had got a bit tense since he stopped being a bird and the laughter helped. Angie's laughter died first. She looked at the author's name again – P P Eineg – and groaned.

'We are soooo thick,' she said.

'Speak for yourself,' I said.

She handed me the book. Pointed at the author's name. Pause. Then I also groaned.

'What is it?' Pete said, leaving the rocker, joining us at the book.

I fingered the Prof's name. Pete spelled it out. Didn't see what we were getting at.

'Try reversing it,' Angie said.

He reversed the name, letter by letter, saying each one out loud. 'Oh yeah,' he said at last. Sounded quite pleased with himself. Then he said it again, less pleased. 'Oh. Yeah.'

JR was leaning against the chest of drawers, thumbs hooked in his pockets, chewing gum. The truth dawned.

'It isn't a genuine book, is it?' I said.

He gave me a cocky grin, then winked at the book, which immediately became a bunch of tulips. Angie's hand shook, but she's made of strong stuff, old Ange.

'Nice,' she said, sniffing the tulips.

'Probably turn into a bucket of snakes any second,' said Pete.

'Eeek!'

She threw the flowers across the room. They

were still in the air when they became a bucket. The bucket landed, and half a dozen snakes slithered out and headed our way. Angie leapt on the bed. There wasn't much room. Pete and I were already there, clinging to one another.

JR did something with his wrist and the snakes disappeared. We got off the bed.

'What are you playing at?' I said.

'Just having a spot of harmless fun, man.'

'Yeah, well it's not appreciated. Go back to the Piddle Pool and wait for the next thousand-and-first pee.'

'The next thousand-and-first pee could be some time coming. I could be down there for another couple of hundred years.'

'At least,' said Pete. 'When the Piddle Pool's under the leisure centre car park you'll be stuck there for good.'

Three shocked heads spun to stare at him. JR was shocked because this was obviously the first he'd heard of it. Angie and I were shocked because the cretin had just handed him our trump card in return for absolutely nothing.

'The Piddle Pool is to be covered over?' JR said.

'After they've filled it in,' said Pete.

JR whirled on me. 'You knew my unnatural habitat was to be destroyed? You knew, and you kept it from me?'

Put like that it sounded kind of mean. 'Must have slipped my mind,' I said.

He sank on to the bed. 'I am betrayed,' he said and burst into tears with his head in his hands. Pete grinned, but I didn't feel too good about this. He looked so pathetic sitting there. Angie must have thought so too because we both went to him, stood either side of him like human bookends, wondering if we should pat him on the back and spout mindless stuff like 'There, there, s'all right, never mind, never mind.' Was it allowed to pat a genie on the back? And if we did would he understand that we were being sympathetic, or would he turn us into something you wouldn't scrape off the sole of your trainer with Bryan Ryan's ruler? So we let him weep, unpatted.

But then JR stopped weeping and looked up at me through his tears.

'Former masters who betray me when they've

had their three wishes are likely to wish for one more thing,' he said.

'Hey Jig, the riddley creep's gonna give you another wish!' said Pete.

'They wish,' JR said, 'that they'd never been born.'

I twitched. Started to jig about nervously.

'I don't know why you're getting so steamed up,' I said. 'You don't want to go back there anyway, you said so yourself.'

'That's not the point. It's been my home for a very long time. How would you like it if someone built a car park over your home?'

'It's not me that's building the car park.'

'You knew about it and didn't tell me, which is worse.'

'I would have told you,' I lied, jigging harder. 'Honest I would, but how many chances have we had for a good old chinwag?'

'Chances enough.' He stood up. He was a lot taller suddenly, a lot broader, a lot older. And kind of dangerous-looking.

I tilted my head to look up at him. 'Hey now, listen, man,' I said, going for cool.

He scowled down at me. 'Don't man me, man.'

I elbowed the cool. 'Anything you say, man.' Went into a Riverdance solo.

'The damage is done,' he said. 'The betrayal is complete. The betrayer must...' He paused, super dramatically.

I gulped. 'Must...?'

He leaned down. His purple eyes, which now matched his hair, glowed into mine.

'*Suffffferrrr,*' he said, slowly, in a very deep unnatural voice.

'S-s-suffer? No, look. I'm a boy. I suffer every day of my life, it's all in the DNA. There's just so much suffering a kid can take, and I'm overdrawn already.'

'I am going to amuse myself with you, ex-Master.'

'Hey, I like a good laugh,' I said, hands on hip, Irish jigging like a loon.

'Then you'll enjoy what I have in mind.'

'What...um...what would that be then?'

He pulled himself up to his new full height, brushing the ceiling with his purple dreads, which were writhing like the bucketful of snakes he'd turned the flowers into.

'You'll find out,' he boomed in this heavy genie voice. 'Tomorrow.'

I glanced at Angie and Pete, who were trying to blend silently with the wallpaper, hoping he'd forget about them. The future was starting to look quite lonely.

'When you say I have to suffer,' I said, 'you do mean just me, right? I mean there are three of us. We're a gang, the Three Musketeers, we share everything. If one of us gets it we all do, one of our little rules.'

'No it isn't,' said Pete.

'One for all and all for lunch?' I said.

'That doesn't mean we all have to be punished for something just *one* of us has done,' said Angie.

'You'd see me face this alone?' They smiled at me. 'I'm shocked,' I said. 'I'm disappointed. I feel...'

'Betrayed?' said JR.

'Exactly.'

'But you have a point,' he said.

'I do?'

'Yes. It seems right that your accomplices

should suffer with you.'

Pete and Angie's smiles fell like bits of cake. I stopped jigging. Felt less lonely already.

'Don't drag us down with you, McCue,' Pete said. 'If this batty crank wants to dump on you, it's nothing to do with us. Leave us out of it.'

'Batty crank?' said JR.

'Short for bats,' I explained.

'Long for bats,' said Angie.

'Means nutty, bonkers, doolally,' said Pete. 'Stark staring out of your genie tree.'

'Bats,' JR rumbled thoughtfully from the ceiling.

The word seemed to amuse him. He still looked amused when he spread his arms like wings and muttered something Mongolian. Then, suddenly, the room was full of...

Bats.

They came at us from the ceiling, the walls, the cupboards, swooping, diving, flapping. We threw ourselves on the floor, hands over our heads. I glanced up once. Fast-moving black shadows everywhere, and JR, back to his usual size, sitting cross-legged in mid-air, inside a big floating bubble. Bats that went for him smacked glass and

106

disappeared with a pop.

The bat invasion probably only lasted two or three minutes, but it felt longer. It ended as suddenly as it started, when JR cried 'Tomorrow!'

Then his bubble burst (with a puff of smoke) and I was left wondering where all this was going to end.

Hey. If only I'd known.

If only I'd *known*!

Chapter Ten

Back home I found that Mum had moved a silly little table over the hole in the carpet. Unfortunately this spoiled the balance of the room in her eyes. Can't bear an unbalanced room, my mother, so she'd moved all the other furniture around to rebalance it, in a different way. This meant that to watch TV from the couch we now had to all look over our left shoulders, or over someone else's shoulder if you were further away. Another thing she'd done while I was gone was hang the Starving Artist painting over the mantelpiece in place of Dad's favourite photo of himself as a boy with his dead father. Couldn't miss it there if you tried. All the wiggly little maggoty shapes made eyes pop and stomachs like mine play leapfrog.

'Oh, Jiggy,' Mum said. 'That cup of tea you made for me earlier.'

'Er... yes?'

'Very distinctive flavour. What was it?'

'Trade secret,' I said. 'But any time you want another one like it, just give me a few minutes' warning.'

When Dad came in and saw that his ancient photo had been put away, he went ballistic. Not a good move. He should know by now that one thing you don't do with my mother is shout at her. The old girl never just sits there and takes it. She jumps right up on her high horse and bawls back, full throttle. In nought to sixty the house was a battleground. I went up to my room and put my headphones on to shut out the parental squawking. Stayed like that for some time and might have stayed like it even longer if the door hadn't burst open to reveal my mother standing in the doorway with wild eyes and an axe. Well, not quite, but I knew she still wasn't in bundle-of-joy mode by the way she ripped the phones from my ears, and shrieked in the nearest one:

'I've been calling you for half an *hour*! Tea – is – READYYYY!!!'

When I went down, the atmosphere between the Golden Oldies was so thick you couldn't have cut it with a chainsaw. Things didn't lighten up much while we ate in total silence either. Even after we finished, the house was as quiet as an Egyptian tomb after grave-robbers have left. Until Dad turned the TV on anyway, with the sound up so loud a person in earmuffs could have heard it three blocks away. Some sporty magazine programme. Usually when sporty stuff is on Dad jumps all over the furniture like a chimp who just sat on a porcupine. Not tonight though. Tonight he perched on the edge of the couch looking over his left shoulder like he'd spent the afternoon at the taxidermist's. Mum kept to other parts of the house, viciously polishing brass. There's a lot of brass in our house. My mother loves the stuff, so we have brass pots, brass jugs, brass horseshoes, brass coasters, brass picture frames – you name it, we have some in brass. I'm only thankful that no-one ever made a brass toilet seat, or we'd have one of those too. And she's a fanatic about seeing her face in it. When my mum's had one of her brass-buffing sessions you daren't go into a room without sunglasses.

I left them to it. My parents could deafen the estate and make the brass gleam without me for an audience. But after twenty minutes up in my room

I was pretty bored. I thought about doing some homework, but not for long, I wasn't that bored. I'd get told off for not doing it, but not by my mother. When I got fed up of doing nothing I went to the window. I looked down. My kennel was still near Mum's rockery, though as I predicted she'd moved it. Not much, just enough for her to feel that it was in the best place until she could think of a way to get shot of it without hurting my feelings. I leaned closer to the glass. It was getting dark, but there seemed to be a glow in the kennel doorway again. Last time I saw a glow there I thought it was because it had been touched by the genie. But here it was again, and brighter than before. As I watched, the glow shifted a little, as if something had moved across the light source. There was something in there! But what? JR? No, couldn't be, he was much too big. But he'd said he might look for a little place of his own. My kennel was a little place. And he could change into anything he wanted. Maybe he'd changed himself into a dog and moved in. Or just made himself smaller to fit. Yes, it was my bet that he was in there, dreaming up a really horrible fate for me, some terrible things

111

to pay me back for not telling him what was going to happen to the Piddle Pool.

I went down for a snack later. To the kitchen, not the kennel. The sound of the TV in the living room was down to human level. I looked in. The old photo was back on the wall and the Starving Artist eye-popper was nowhere to be seen. Dad had won. He was snoring on the couch with his head on his left shoulder, arms folded round a cushion. Mum had turned her chair away so she wouldn't have to look at him. She was watching a documentary about divorce.

I went to the kitchen. Paused in the doorway. The hall light caught the gleam of the newly polished ornamental brass coal scuttle just inside the door. I took a deep breath and flipped the light switch. The reason for the pause and the deep breath is that the strip light in our kitchen isn't like other strip lights. When you turn it on you stand there blinking like crazy for at least thirty seconds before it settles down. Gives a whole new meaning to something being on the blink. After these thirty seconds you usually have such a blinding headache that you can't remember why you came in, and you

112

take a couple of paracetamol and totter off to another room to give them a chance to work. I didn't get a headache this time, but I should have because every time the light flashed I was dazzled by super-brilliant brass all over the kitchen. It's a wonder my pupils didn't overheat.

I made my little snack.* While wolfing it, my gaze drifted to the window. All I could see was my own reflection surrounded by gleaming brass, so I turned the light off. I leaned over the sink and pressed my nose against the glass. With the light off you couldn't miss the glow from the kennel – or what was leaning against it: the Starving Artist painting. Typical of my mother. All or nothing with her. If she can't have something exactly where she wants it, she'll sling it. Next stop after the kennel for the maggoty masterpiece would be the wheely bin. She wouldn't get any argument from me about *that*.

I was still thinking all this when a green face surrounded by spookily dancing dreadlocks slithered up the window and winked at me. My healthy little snack hit the ceiling. I screamed and shot backwards. There was an almighty crash as I

---

* Bowl of cereal, four slices of toast with strawberry jam and peanut butter, tub of Bill & Ben's Luxury Ice-cream, bag of salt and vinegar crisps, jammy doughnut, Diet Cola. (Fortunately, all the liquids had gone back to normal by this time.)

landed on something hard. The almighty crash was followed by an almighty shout from the living room. The almighty shout was followed by the sound of running slippers, which only stopped when the nation's favourite brass buffer hurtled in and flipped the light switch. I bucked and writhed and shuddered on the floor for the full thirty blinking seconds before hauling myself into a sitting position and looking to see what I'd fallen on: the ornamental brass coal scuttle, which now had a dent as big as a horse's buttock.

'Well at least it's still shiny,' I said.

Some time later, when my mother finally stopped lashing me with her tongue, I plodded wearily up to bed. I lay awake for some time thinking about the winker at the window. That wink told me that I was in for a pretty rough time tomorrow, so it's probably not surprising that when I eventually fell asleep I had another nightmare. Once again it wasn't about JR, though. Nor what he'd got lined up for me. I was walking into my mother's Starving Artist painting, and as I walked in all the wiggly little multicoloured shapes came to life. And the life they came to was…maggots. Yes, maggots again. All around me they were, then all over me, wiggling into my ears, my nose, all my personal nooks and crannies, and…

You've heard people say that something makes their flesh crawl? Well in my sleep, in my second maggoty nightmare, those horrible little beasts made my flesh crawl. I mean *literally*.

Chapter Eleven

Morning. I didn't wait for my mother to wear her throat out shouting for me to get up. I was awake and alert as soon as I heard her trudging wearily downstairs to open the curtains and slam some doors. I opened my eyes. Cautiously, nervously. This was the day JR was going to make my life a misery, and I had no idea what to expect. I raised my head and took in the room. My clothes hung from the lampshade! My school books were thrown all over the place! My carpet was all rucked up! My curtains hung like rags! The posters on the walls were torn or peeling off!

I breathed a sigh of relief. Everything as normal.

I rolled out of bed and went to the bathroom. I flipped the toilet seat up, sprayed the dried flower arrangement beside the pan, re-aimed, soaked away half the Loo Blue, dropped the lid, flushed, and went to the basin to wash my hands like a good boy. While rinsing the mitts I checked the McCue features in the mirror. The McCue features were as dashing and handsome as ever, with one slight difference. There was something missing above the eyebrows.

I was bald!

Totally, hopelessly, hideously bald!

I looked like Mr Prior, my neurotic RE teacher. Prior is bald. Super bald. His head rises upwards from his ears like an extinct volcano. But at least he has the odd little wisp of hair here and there. I didn't. Not one wisp. I gripped the edge of the basin and did some simple breathing exercises. Not so simple after all. I tried again, got a breath, hung on to it. I'd tried to imagine what JR had in mind for me, but nothing had come close to this. Total baldness! How do you handle that? I mean what does a person do when his skull is on the outside? Mr Prior would know. Or perhaps not. Perhaps that's why he's so neurotic.

My first thought, once I started to get used to my new look, was that there was no way I could go to school hairless. My second thought was that if I bunked off once more this term they'd carry out their threat and insert me in the offal grinder in the school kitchen. And there wasn't only school to think about. There were my parents. If I cancanned past them with a jolly 'Morning Ma, morning Pa, and how are we today?' they might just notice that my parting was a little wider than usual. I wound a towel round my head and left the bathroom.

'Hi, Jig. What's with the towel?'

Dad. I checked his eyes. Normal bloodshot, not purple. The Real McCue.

'Washed my hair,' I said.

'You what? You never wash your hair.'

'New Year's Resolution.'

'It's nowhere near New Year.'

'Old resolution, just got round to it.'

We banged doors at opposite ends of the landing.

In my room I began to shake. Delayed shock. When I was all shaken out, I touched my head with my fingertips. Smooth as a beach ball. Horrible. I got dressed, then cranked the door back a centimetre to peer out. All clear. Raised voices down in the kitchen. My parents were talking again. Well, bickering. They were both still in the doghouse with each other, but they'd missed their chance. Unless I'd got it wrong, the doghouse was taken. I left my room and peered over the banister. In the hall below, just inside the front door, we have a big coat rack. On the coat rack, as well as a couple of coats, are the second-hand hats Dad buys at *Help the Aged*. He doesn't wear these hats, just collects them. There's a cricket hat for not playing cricket, a fishing hat for not fishing, a deerstalker for not stalking deer, a porkpie for not eating pork pies, a derby for not going racing, a baseball cap for not playing baseball, and a woolly bobble hat for doing nothing at all. One of these could be useful to me, but it was all the way down there by the kitchen, which contained my parents. I swung the towel round my head again and did a lightning tiptoe down the stairs, missing the third, fifth, ninth and eleventh, which creak. New house and the stairs creak. Until we moved here I thought you only got creaky stairs in old places. Dad says you do, unless your new house is built by cowboys.

Creeeeaaaak!

Whoops, forgot about stair twelve. The sniping in the kitchen stopped. I bounded across the hall, threw the towel aside, jammed the nearest hat on my head and pulled it down as far as it would go. Unfortunately this wasn't very far because I'd grabbed the bowler, but no one came out, so I was able to switch to the woolly bobble hat. I hauled it over my ears. No one would suspect that I was as shiny as a new spoon under all that old knitting.

I went into the kitchen. Into complete silence. Mum was standing at the toaster watching bread burn and Dad sat at the table not laughing at the cartoons in the paper. It was obvious why they'd gone quiet. Mum had heard the twelfth stair and told Dad to shut up. She doesn't think parents should argue in front of their kids. I heard her scream that at Dad one day from the next room. They didn't even glance up as I went in, but they soon would, and then they'd notice the headgear. So I got in first.

'Dad, can I borrow your hat?'

He glanced up. 'Which hat?'

'This one.'

'Why?'

'It's Wear-A-Hat-For-Charity Day at school.'

'That's a new one.'

'Yeah. Teachers. Nothing else to think about.'

'Where does the charity come in?' Mum asked from the smoking toaster.

'Parents make donations in return for the school allowing the kids to wear hats for the day.'

'*Allowing?*' Dad said. 'It's supposed to be a *favour*?'

'How much?' Mum said.

'Up to you.'

The black toast jumped out of the toaster with a scowl and Mum snatched her purse from the dresser.

'I'll see to it,' Dad said.

Mum froze. Stared at him. Dad never volunteers to pay for stuff. He reached in his trouser pocket, slapped a handful of change on the table, and sorted through. He flipped me a coin. The smallest one.

'Is that all you're going to give him?' Mum said.

'It's only for charity.'

Mum said one of those words she's always telling Dad not to say in my hearing and emptied her purse on the table. Gave me one that really *was* worth something.

'No, that's too much,' I said, coming over all guilty.

121

'I won't have people saying the McCues are skinflints,' she said. 'Even if one of us is.'

I shovelled some cereal down my neck, left the kitchen, and tripped over the towel I'd left on the hall floor. I snatched up the towel and headed upstairs. On the landing I took the phone off the wall and into the bathroom. Pushed buttons.

'Yeah?' Pete.

'Is Angie about?'

'Might be, who wants to know?'

'Come on, stop messing about, get Ange.'

'Why, what's up?'

'I'll tell her.'

'Tell me, I'll tell her.'

'No, Pete, I'll tell her, then maybe she'll tell you or maybe she won't, her decision.'

'I'll remember that next time I phone your place,' he said.

'Remember what? Not to tell me stuff? So who will you tell instead? My mum? My dad? Stallone?'

'*Angieeee!*' he yelled, half deafening me. While he was waiting for her, he said, 'Don't think I've forgotten yesterday either.'

'Don't think *I've* forgotten,' I said.

'I've not forgotten as much as you.'

'Yeah, well I've forgotten even less than you.'

'Want a bet?'

'How much?'

'How much you got?'

'Nothing.'

'I'll double it.'

There was a scuffling sound, then a different voice came on: 'Jig?'

'Angie, listen,' I said. 'Got a problem.'

'Story of your life.'

'Yeah. Need to talk to you.'

'You are talking to me.'

'Face to face. Minus Pete. Something to show you.'

'Something to show me but not Pete? Interesting.'

'Don't want to see anyway,' said Pete in the background.

'Can you come over?' I said.

'Just me?' said Ange.

'Just you.'

'OK, soon as I've been to the bathroom.'

'How soon will that be?'

'What do you want, a timetable?'

She clicked off.

I passed my toothbrush near my teeth, adjusted the *Help the Aged* bobble, and left the bathroom. I started downstairs just as my father started up. As we approached he gave the hat a smirk.

'Prat,' he said.

'Ditto,' I replied. 'But at least I can take the hat off.'

I slipped out to the back garden and approached the kennel. If JR was in there I planned to fall flat on my face and promise to worship him to the end of my days if only he'd give me my hair back. I got down and looked in the doggy doorway. No genie, in any shape, size or form. But the inside of the kennel was something else.

It was twenty times bigger than it was on the outside!

The walls and ceiling were far enough apart for a full grown teenage-size genie to play hopscotch in. And it was furnished. There was a fancy carpet, wardrobe, table and chairs, four-poster bed and on one of the walls...the Starving Artist painting that

Mum had put out. JR must have seen it leaning against the kennel, taken a shine to it, and bunged it on the wall of his adopted home.

I was still staring in through the little doorway when something nudged my arm. I went cold. Turned to look. A mean furry face close to mine, eyes like green ice. I moved aside. Slowly. You have to watch how you move around Stallone or he'll take your ears off. When I was out of the way he took a peek in the kennel. Unlike me, he didn't seem very amazed. Maybe cats don't do amazed. He started to go in.

'No, Stal, don't, it's not yours.'

He looked back at me, snarled, then went all the way in. You just can't tell that cat. I ducked down to see what he did next. He went straight to the four-poster bed, jumped up on it, sprawled out, closed his eyes.

'Well you're a braver cat than I am,' I said, and left him to it.

Chapter Twelve

I'd been looking out for Angie and was at the door before she could ring the bell. 'What's with the stupid hat?' she said as I pulled her inside.

'Tell you in a—'

'Hello, Angie, you're early.'

My mother. She doesn't miss much.

'Jiggy wanted to see me,' Angie told her.

'Need advice, homework thing,' I said.

'Oh.' Mum immediately lost interest: nothing to do with her these days, homework. 'No hat, Angie?'

'Hat?' said Ange.

'I thought you all had to wear one today.'

'Only if you have kind parents who give money to charity,' I said quickly.

'Ah.' She looked pleased, and went into the kitchen.

Angie dropped her school bag and we headed upstairs.

'What was that about?'

'Wait.'

I went into my room and closed the door. Then I opened it again and let Angie in. She screwed her face up and fell back against the wall.

'Don't you ever open *windows* in here?'

'Mum's job, like making the beds and tidying up after everyone.'

'You may not have heard,' she scowled, 'but women are equal to men. Actually they're superior, but they still get all the bum jobs.'

'Angie, listen. You know JR? You know what he said about paying me back for not telling him the Piddle Pool is all set to go under a car park?'

'Yes…'

'Well it's started.'

'What's started?'

I hooked my thumbs in the rim of the woolly bobble hat that covered my head and most of my ears.* I raised it, slowly, bit by bit. For each bit Angie's mouth dropped two, until her jaw was on her chest.

'What…?' she said when my full glory was revealed. 'What…?'

'Couldn't have put it better myself,' I replied.

---

* Well, two of them.

'Your hair. It's…gone.'

'Yes.'

'But, Jig, you're…bald.'

'That's what happens when the hair goes.'

'Yerp!' she said, or something like it, and shuddered from head to foot.

'Now you know why the stupid hat,' I said, tugging it back on.

'And you think JR did that?'

'No, Ange, I think we had a burglar last night who secretly wants to be a barber.'

'Who knows about this?'

'Just you and me so far.'

'Oh, Pete will have a field day.'

'Which is why I had to tell you first. Need to build up to the devastating Garrett wit.'

'You'll never hear the end of it. And not just from him. Do you realise you have to go to *school* like that?'

I sank miserably on to my bed. 'I realise.'

'Show me again,' she said.

'No. You shuddered.'

'You caught me off guard. I know what to expect now.'

I took the hat off. She shuddered from head to foot. I pulled the hat on again. I was starting to wish I'd kept it to myself.

'Well it takes some getting used to,' she said. 'Tell you what, though, you haven't half got a big head without hair.'

'Thanks for that,' I said. 'Now I won't have to worry about people staring at my no-hairline. They'll be too busy spreading the word about the size of my *bonce*.'

The doorbell went in the distance.

'Pete,' said Angie.

'Still not ready for him.'

'Ready or not, time to go. What are you going to do about the head?'

'Keep the hat on.'

'Jig, no teacher's going to let you wear a hat in class.'

'I'll make something up. Like I contracted this contagious scalp disease overnight that'll spread like crazy if I take it off.'

'And the hat's lined with lead so the contagion won't leak through the *wool*? Oh yes, I can see them falling for that.'

Mum was at the front door talking to Pete when we went down.

'What's this about having to wear a hat?' he said, eyeing mine.

Angie and I grabbed our bags and crowded him off the step.

'Trouble with you,' I said, very loudly, 'is you don't listen when teachers tell you stuff.'

'Old habits die hard,' Pete said.

'Have a nice day!' Mum cried as we dragged our bags up the path.

'Yeah, right,' I said. 'I'm really looking forward to this one.'

Pete didn't take the baldy head the way I thought he would. When I told him he wanted a peek, naturally, so I hoiked the hat about half way so all the Peeping Toms and Traceys on the estate wouldn't simultaneously faint and crash through their windows. Pete didn't fall down in hysterics. He screwed his chops up and backed away.

'Jig, that's...that's... Errrk!'

'It's no worse than Mr Prior's,' I said. 'Give or take a wisp.'

'Prior's always been like that, only way we've

ever known him, but you, you've always had hair, and... God! I'm not sitting next to *you* today!'

With these touching words of support he scooted on ahead, shuddering with every other step.

The closer we got to the shopping centre the more kids appeared. Some made smart remarks about the hat, but most didn't bother. People often wear something loopy to school for a laugh and take it off when they get there, so as not to get in trouble. What they had yet to find out was that the hat was staying.

Morning registration wasn't a problem. It only takes five minutes and I was able to use the kids in front as a shield while Mr Dakin called the register. After registration though, we had History with Hurley, and Mr Hurley misses nothing. He's short and stocky and he has a head like a big rubber bullet and a very thick neck that bulges over his collar. He always wears a check sports jacket and brown cavalry twills, and the same dark red tie with a little badge woven into it. He once told us that the tie was a club tie, but he didn't say which club, or even what sort of club, mainly because nobody asked or cared less. Mr Hurley doesn't really want to teach us, you can tell. Goes out of his way to make his lessons super boring. Other teachers use things like video and TV to try and get us interested but Hurley just talks at us, very straight, very serious, and writes stuff on the blackboard for us to copy down silently. The only laughs we get are when he writes on the board. Hurley-Burley's blackboard is quite a tall one, and when he stretches up to write on the top his jacket rises, giving us a cheeky view of his rear end in the shiny seat of his twills. We fire pretend arrows at it, hold our noses, and cover our mouths to keep the joy in. Yes, I know, pretty infantile, but with teachers that boring you take what you can get.

Pete and I sit right at the back in History, hoping Hurley won't notice us, pick on us, ask us stuff to prove we've been paying attention, you know the kind of thing. I'd got into the classroom without him seeing me, walking behind others with my knees bent, all the way to my seat, where I scrunched down as low as I could. Most of the kids were pretty amused by my hat, but they stopped pointing and hooting when Mr H told them to shut up. He was standing on tiptoe writing on the top half of the board and flashing his shiny bum when someone who shall remain nameless – Bryan Ryan – blew the whistle on me. Hurley had just written about these ancient nomadic desert dwellers having a job surviving because it was so cold at night when Ryan saw his chance.

'You want to ask McCue if *he's* feeling the cold, sir. In his *head*.'

The Hurley hand froze on the chalk – he hates being interrupted when he's writing on the board – but then carried on to the end of the boring sentence before turning round.

'Who was that?'

'Ryan,' said half a dozen sneaks, including Pete.

Hurley turned his bullet head slowly in Ryan's direction.

'And what did Ryan say?' he asked. Ryan didn't answer. 'Stand up, Ryan.' Ryan stood up. 'Well?' Hurley said.

'Yes, thanks, sir. You?'

'What was it you said about McCue just then?'

'Didn't say nothing, sir.'

133

'Didn't say *anything*,' said Mr Hurley.

'That's right, sir, you've got it.'

Hurley looked as if his neck might spill over his collar and become an extra shoulder, but he managed to hold it in.

'Sit down, Ryan, you wear me out.'

'Do my best, sir.'

The Boring History Teacher of the Year looked as if he was going to leave it at that and half turned back to his shivering desert dwellers. But then he changed his mind and half turned round again.

'Mr McCue,' he said, standing on tiptoe and lifting his chin to see over all the heads between him and me. Everyone in the line of fire shrank helpfully down in their seats to give him a clear view. He could no longer miss the huddled Help the Aged bobble. '*Are* you feeling the cold in your head, McCue?'

'Mm,' I said.

'Care to elaborate?'

'It's this thing I get sometimes. The doc says I have to keep my head covered or I could get pneumonia and die.'

'Ah. Then you'll have a note.'

'Note?'

'If the doctor has seen you and made this startling pronouncement he will presumably have written a note for you to bring to school. Such a note would apprise me of the facts, so that I might avoid making the mistake of asking you to remove the headwear in the misguided belief that you are telling a pack of porkies.'

'I left it at home,' I said.

'Left what at home?'

'The note.'

'So there is a note?'

'Yeah, sure, course.'

'And you'll bring it in tomorrow if the condition persists?'

'Count on it.'

'In the meantime, however, until the note is presented, I would be *immensely* grateful if you would discard that...article.'

'But if I take it off I might die, sir.'

'We'll just have to take a chance on that, won't we?'

'I can't, sir.'

'You can, sir. You'd better, sir.'

'No, I can't – really. I'll bring the note tomorrow, promise.'

I'll get Pete to do one for me tonight, I thought. If Pete's good for anything at all it's forging documents on his PC.

But Mr Hurley wasn't having it.

'If you don't take that thing off,' he said, 'you will be paying a visit to the Head.'

'He's already got a head, sir!' shouted Eejit Atkins. 'That's where he keeps the hat!'

This didn't do much for Sir's mood. In fact it sent it into a nosedive.

'McCue! Hat! Remove!'

I glanced around. Everyone was looking at me to see what I'd do next. Even Pete, sitting as far away as anyone can when they're right next to you, had one eye on me.

'Can't be done,' I said. 'Sorry, but there you go.'

All this time, Mr Hurley had remained at the front beside the blackboard. But now he put his chalk down, dusted his hands, and headed my way. His neck was bulging so much over his collar that it looked like it might burst and spatter us with neck stuff. Then he was standing over me, looking down at me. His eyes were very cold. He'd obviously spent too much time with freezing nomads.

'Are you defying me, McCue?'

He said it very quietly, almost gently, but I still didn't like the sound of it. I made one last attempt.

'I don't want to, sir, really I don't, only if I take the hat off there's no telling what'll happen.'

'Remove it,' he said, not quite so gently.

'I can't *do* that,' I said. He was really starting to get to me. 'That's the *point*. That's what I'm *saying*. The hat has to *stay*!'

I slumped even further down in my seat and folded my arms. Closed my eyes to shut him out.

'Right,' I heard him say.

'Yeah, right,' I said, eyes still closed.

'Jig!'

Urgent whisper from Pete. I opened my eyes just in time to see Mr Hurley reaching for my bobble. My hand shot up and grabbed his wrist. His fingers went rigid, just short of the hat. The class gasped. Hurley twisted his wrist out of my powerful grip.

'The Head's office. Now!'

I got up, keeping well away from him in case he

made another grab at the hat. But he stepped back, let me by. I shoved my hands in my pockets and mooched towards the door. All eyes were on me, I could feel them. For the first time I felt ridiculous in the *Help the Aged* bobble.

Chapter Thirteen

To get to the Head you have to get past Miss Prince, his minder. Miss Prince is a very large lady who always wears black leggings. There's nothing else to say about her really. When I strolled into her personal office space she was watering a bonsai tree with an eye dropper.

'I have to see Mr Hubbard,' I said.

'He's at the dentist's, I'm afraid.'

'Has he got a note?'

'Excuse me?'

'Any idea how long he'll be?'

'Hard to say. What do you mean, a note?'

'Do I wait or come back?' I said.

'Up to you. Joseph McCue, isn't it?'

'No.'

'Shall I tell him you were looking for him Joseph?'

'No.'

She looked at my hat.

'Is there something wrong with your head?'

'Probably,' I said, and vamoosed.

It's always a relief to be walking away from Mother Hubbard's office, even when you know you have to go back soon. But now I had a decision to make. Return to Mr Hurley's class for the rest of his boring lesson or hang about somewhere else till the next one. Guess which I went for. The trouble with hanging about during school time though, specially on school premises, is that you have to keep away from the prying eyes of teachers. There's always one or two loping along the corridors trying to look like they're doing something useful when they don't have a lesson.

'What are you doing out of class, McCue?!'

Like now. He saw me even before he came round the corner, I swear he did, and suddenly there he was, the Man in Red, Ranting Lane's very own Superhero.

'Been to see Mr Hubbard, sir.'

'Why?!' he shouted. Mr Rice always shouts. 'Up to no good again?!'

'Bound to be, you know what these headteachers are like.'

By this time he was up close, squinting

suspiciously at the *Help the Aged* bobble.

'What's with the hat, McCue?!'

'Hat? What hat?'

His head started to throb, the way it does when he's annoyed. It often throbs when he's near me for some reason.

'Go away, boy! Run along before I lose my *temper*!'

'No running in the corridors,' I said, and put a swift corner between us.

The Boys' toilets seemed the best place to pass some time, so I made a beeline for the nearest. I breezed in, saw the mop and bucket and brown coat of Mr Heathcliff, our depressed caretaker, and breezed out again. As I breezed I turned round – and almost had a heart attack. When you leave somewhere you're not supposed to be, the last person you want to meet is someone who looks like he bumps off bad kids for the Mob in his lunch hour.

'Everything all right?' Mr Flowerdew asked as I patted my heart.

'Will be,' I replied. 'Soon as the pacemaker kicks in.'

He adjusted his dark glasses, sniffed the flower

in his buttonhole, said, 'Good,' and went on his way. Funny old cove, Flowerdew.

Where now? I wasn't sure, but I couldn't just stand around outside the Boys'. I scooted through the corridors in search of a hiding place, running low every time I came to the windows or glass-topped door of a classroom. There were a lot of these, far too many. Every time I heard adult voices that weren't in a classroom, I shot off down another corridor.

Ranting Lane is a big school, and it's kind of like a maze, and after a while, running with my head down, I found myself in a corridor I didn't recognise. At the end of it was a door I didn't recognise either, but then I saw green through the glass above the exit bar and realised this was the side of the school where the playing fields are. I didn't want the playing fields, so I flipped round. I was about to shoot off in some other direction when I heard voices round the corner ahead. No choice then. I ran to the exit door, lifted the bar, slipped out. Then I squatted down on the other side, and peeked up through the glass just as a couple of teachers turned into the corridor.

'Hello, young Jiggy. On the run, are we?'

I groaned. Pesky teachers, everywhere you go. I turned round, still crouching. It was Mr Dent, the Woodwork honcho, so it could have been worse. Mr Dent wasn't like your usual teacher. He talked to us like we were human. You could even swear in front of him so long as you didn't do it too often. Still, he was one of Them. I did a quick dash through the rubble in my head looking for a decent lie, but my brain seemed to be on a lie break and I couldn't find one. So I told him the truth. Most of it. About Mr Hurley getting mad because I wouldn't lose the hat and sending me to Mr Hubbard. About Hubbard being at the dentist. About not wanting to go back to Hurley's lesson. About trying to keep out of the way till the next class. He nodded understandingly.

'And the reason for the hat is…?'

This was the one thing I hadn't mentioned. And I couldn't. It would have meant going through the whole genie thing, and no adult would believe that, even Mr Dent.

'Mind if I skip that, sir?'

He shrugged. And that was it. No pressure, no commands, no threats.

'Want to give me a hand?' he said. 'If you're helping me and someone sees you, I can always say I asked you to.'

I'd been squatting against the door all this time so I wouldn't be seen by the teachers on the other side. I looked through the glass. No sign. They must have gone into a room off the corridor.

I stood up. 'Hand with what?'

'Bagging sawdust.'

'Huh?'

He led the way to the old Woodwork shop. The old Woodwork shop hadn't been used for months. The one we used now was in a new extension, with new workbenches and mostly new equipment. The new shop looks out on other parts of the school, which isn't very interesting. The old one looked right across the playing fields, and there were trees around the edge, and it was all open and spacious. I used to spend a lot of time daydreaming at the old Woodwork shop windows and it was kind of unreal going back there. The benches and stools and most of the old vices and lathes and stuff had been carted away for scrap, or sold off, so it was pretty empty. Even smelt different.

'Weird,' I said as we went in.

'Yes,' Mr Dent said. 'I quite liked this old hovel.'

He led the way to a big barrel of sawdust in the corner and handed me a small brown sack and a trowel. I wondered what I was supposed to do with them until he started scooping sawdust out of the barrel with another trowel into another sack. For as long as I'd been at Ranting Lane the Woodwork sawdust had been swept up at the end of lessons and dumped in this barrel. I'd never given it a thought, and suddenly here I was scooping the sawdust out again, into a sack.

'What's it for?' I asked.

'The pet hypermarket. They pay a pittance for it, then flog it for a vastly inflated profit to people with rabbits and hampsters and such.'

'Doesn't the school mind?'

'Mind what?'

'You selling school sawdust to the pet hypermarket.'

'This isn't a private scam,' he said. 'The few pennies we make go into petty cash to pay for a jar or two of cheap and nasty coffee for the staffroom.'

He finished filling his sack, sealed the top with

wire, and started on another while my first was only a quarter full. He'd been with us about two years, Mr Dent, and we only had him for an hour a week, so I didn't know him too well, and when silence fell – almost at once – I found it a bit uncomfortable. He seemed OK with it though. Kept breaking into a whistle.

Mr Dent had two very unusual features. One was his eyes. His eyes were so incredibly blue that they looked like he'd borrowed them from a cartoon character. The other unusual feature was the dent in his forehead. Yes, his name was Dent and he had a dent in his head, as if he'd chosen one to go with the other. It looked like he'd spent the first few years of his life leaning his head on the end of a broom handle. We used to make jokes about Dent's dent behind his back, but once we discovered what a nice bloke he was we stopped. Most of us anyway.

After a while, because there's just so much whistling and silence I can take, I said: 'Do you like teaching Woodwork, sir?'

He glanced up from his little sack of sawdust.

'It's a job. Pays the bills.'

'But you don't actually like it?'

146

'Oh, I like it well enough. It's not quite as colourful as my old profession, but there are worse ways of earning a living.'

'What was your old profession?'

He frowned at me, and for a sec I thought he was going to tell me to stop being so nosy, but he didn't. He put his trowel down, and reached behind my left ear. When he opened his hand there was an egg in it. Then the egg cracked and a small beak popped out.

'Uh?' I said.

Before I could see what the beak belonged to Mr Dent dropped the egg in his pocket.

'Just a trick,' he said.

'Hey! You mean you used to be a *magician*?'

He smiled and picked up his trowel again. 'Something of the sort.'

'Wow. Why did you give it up?'

'Question of economics. There's not much call for my sort of show these days.'

'So you became a Woodwork teacher.'

'Well, first I became a Turkish carpet salesman. I was rather good at that. The carpets just *flew* out of the shop when I was on duty.'

'Flying carpets...' I smiled, thinking about JR believing that Mr Dent was a genie.

'But in spite of my brilliant salesmanship, the firm went out of business, so...'

'You became a Woodwork teacher.'

'I became a Woodwork teacher.'

I noticed that his amazingly blue eyes had gone all moist. Must be quite an emotional thing, I thought, looking back to the good old days when you performed magic tricks on stage for cheering audiences. He bent his head and carried on scooping sawdust from the barrel.

'Tell me about being a magician,' I said.

I was really interested. I'd never met a magician in the flesh before. I'd seen a few on stage or the telly, but I'd never actually met one.

'Rather not,' Mr Dent said. 'Another life.'

'So you never do the act at all now?' I said.

'I still do the odd gig, just small stuff, little private functions. Got one tonight as a matter of... Blast it!'

'What's up?'

'One of my contacts fell out.'

'Contacts?'

'Lenses.'

'Is this another trick, sir?'

'No, it's not another trick,' he said irritably. 'I've dropped a flipping contact in the sawdust.'

'I didn't know you wore contact lenses.'

He peered into the barrel.

'Have done for years. Can't see a thing without them.'

He started sifting carefully through the sawdust.

'Can't see it,' I said, looking, not sifting.

He sifted some more, like someone panning for gold. Then:

'Ah!'

He opened his fist. In his palm was a little blue sawdusty disc. He went to the big white sink in the corner. Just as he turned the tap on to rinse the contact, I felt a shiver in the air. JR materialised at my elbow. He looked kind of agitated.

'Oh, it's you,' I whispered. 'Where's my hair?'

'Never mind your hair, you have to hide me. He mustn't see me!'

'Who mustn't see you?'

'The genie! I don't think he's sensed me yet. He might not if we're quick!'

149

I glanced at Mr Dent bending over the sink with his back to us, rinsing his contact. The Woodwork teacher who doubled as a genie. Hard not to laugh out loud, but I played along.

'What do you need me for? Vanish. Become a slug or a bendy straw or something.'

'I can't do any of that,' he said. 'Not right now.'

'How come?'

'Can we go into this later? I'm a bit pushed for time here.'

I smiled at him. He twitched. He had to tell me, he knew.

'All right, all right. When two genies get this close, they lose power. I have about as much magic right now as a pet rabbit.'

'Well you knew he'd be somewhere in school,' I said. 'What did you come for if you're so bothered about him?'

'Thought I'd take a chance. I wanted to see how you were...you know...handling the hair thing.'

'You mean have a gloat.'

'Well... Look, just hide me, we'll talk later. Please?'

You could tell from the angle of Mr D's elbows that he was slotting his contact back in place. He'd turn round any second. JR was shaking. I didn't feel very sympathetic.

'Give me my hair back first.'

'No,' he said. 'Not yet. You haven't suffered enough.'

'No deal then,' I said.

'No deal?'

'If you won't fix my hair, I'm not helping you.'

I don't know what I expected him to do, flee in panic maybe. But he didn't do that. He gave a snort of fury and dived into the sawdust barrel – seconds before Mr Dent turned round and came towards me with his two bright blue eyes and one wet cheek. He noticed the sawdust all around the barrel that hadn't been there before JR jumped in.

'What happened here?'

I was about to say the first thing that came into my head, when...

'Alan, have you seen Miss Weeks? She's got the key to the Dangerous Explosives cupboard.'

Mr Flowerdew leant in the door, all pale and shaky, like yesterday.

'Miss Weeks?' Mr Dent said. 'No. Haven't seen her for weeks.' He beamed. 'I've been wanting to say that ever since she joined our merry throng.' He saw that we weren't laughing. 'Sorry,' he said, clearing his throat and putting a serious face on. 'Last I saw of her, Vic, she was on her way to the gym, around half nine.'

Mr F thanked him and tottered off.

'Nice fella, old Flowerdew,' Mr Dent said, 'but I wish he'd lighten up a bit.'

'He doesn't look very well,' I said.

'Needs a trip to the Costa del Knees-up, same as me.'

I glanced at the clock on the wall. 'Gotta go, sir. English.'

'Right oh. Thanks for the help.'

'I didn't do much.'

He looked at the one bag I'd filled to his three.

'That's true,' he said.

I started for the door. But stopped. When he started trowelling sawdust again he'd find JR cowering in the barrel. What then? JR thought Mr D was a genie and he didn't want anything to do with other genies. He might lash out, and because

152

Mr Dent wasn't really a genie he might end up as pet litter himself. What to do? Tell my Woodwork teacher there was a genie in the sawdust barrel? He'd think I was crazy, but probably take a look anyway. And then...

As it happened I didn't have to do anything, because just then Mr Dent coughed, and said: 'I could do with a break myself. Not good for the lungs, this stuff.'

We stepped outside and headed in different directions. I peered in the old workshop windows as I passed. Saw JR rise from the barrel, dreadlocks shaking sawdust every which way. I ducked before he could see me. Shot away.

Chapter Fourteen

When I joined the others fighting to be last into English they greeted me like a conquering hero. Far as they knew I'd reported to Mother Hubbard and won the Battle of the Hat, because I was still wearing it. There were no questions *why* I was wearing it. They knew why. I was Defying Authority. Stuff like that always goes down well with my class. Specially the boys. Even Ryan raised a thumb at me. I got quite a bang out of all the attention actually.

I'm good at just two things at school: English and Art. Words and pictures, a breeze. My English teacher, Mrs Gamble, is pretty ancient – about fifty – and there are more lines on her face than a Roman road map. She doesn't take kindly to people fooling around too much in her lessons, but I hardly ever do. No, seriously. I like her and I like her subject, so I behave myself. Usually.

She waved to us as she came in. Glanced at my

hat, shook her head, raised her eyes to the ceiling, but didn't mention it. When she'd got us quiet, she started telling us something or other about 'language'. Don't ask me what, I was so high on my popularity by then that all I was interested in was making myself even more popular – with the kids, not the teaching staff. And the quickest way to do that was...

'Hey miss, liven it up, eh, we're having trouble keeping awake here.'

She stopped what she was saying.

'Thanks for telling me, Jiggy, I wouldn't want to *bore* you.'

'Make sure you don't,' I said.

Cheers all round. Mrs Gamble smiled and started again.

But I wasn't done yet. Fifteen or twenty words later I said: 'Could you speak up, miss? Project the old voice? It's kinda hard to catch the really fascinating stuff you're spouting.'

Her smile was a little weaker this time.

'Settle down now, Jiggy. We have a lot to get through.'

I settled down. I didn't want to ruin my terrific

reputation with one of my favourite teachers. So it came as quite a surprise – to me as well as everyone else – when my hand suddenly went back over my shoulder and lobbed a blackboard rubber down the room. Blackboard rubber? How had a blackboard rubber got into my hand? Luckily Mrs G saw it coming and threw herself across her desk just in time. Missed her by a wrinkle.

Everyone was too stunned to cheer this time, including me, including Mrs Gamble, who got up off the desk, smoothing her dress down.

'Jiggy?' she said.

I opened my mouth to say, 'Sorry, miss, don't know what happened there,' but different words came out. These:

'What's the problem, you miserable old trout?'

Again no cheers, though someone giggled nervously. Eejit Atkins, I think. Mrs Gamble stared at me with this slightly hurt expression.

'What is the matter with you today?'

Words of apology formed in my brain. I trundled them down to my tonsils, arranged them on my tongue, parted my lips, and said:

'Nothing's the matter with me, you old windbag.

But I'm not the one with a face like the back end of a donkey and a voice like a castrated orang-utan.'

Yes, these are the very words that jerked out of the McCue speech-hole. I wasn't responsible for them, of course, but for a minute even I didn't realise where else they could have come from. No, not a minute, about three seconds. And if I needed proof...

'So you wouldn't help me, eh?' a voice said in my ear.

I glanced over my shoulder, first this one, then that. No one behind either of them apart from my adoring fans and some girls. No one visible.

'Hey, come on,' I whispered to nothing. 'Don't drop me in it here.'

'Now what are you up to?' Mrs Gamble demanded from the front.

'Go boil your head in a bucket of mud,' I said.

'Oh my giddy aunt.' This was Angie, from some desks away.

'What are you *doing*, Jig?' (Pete, who hadn't cottoned on yet.)

I leaned over. 'He's here,' I whispered.

'Who is?'

'*Him!*'

'Oh, you mean...' He looked around. 'Can't see him.'

'Take it from me, he's here.'

'Jiggy, would you come here please?'

Mrs Gamble was glaring at me. I got up, eager to please and be one of her favourites again.

'On my way, you ancient bloodsucker.'

'Jiggy, shut your *trap*!' Angie hissed, in the nicest possible way.

I shut it, hard. The class was very quiet as I headed for the front, lips clamped to stop them letting dangerous stuff out. I couldn't hold them for long though. It was as if two tiny hands, one per lip, seized hold and pulled them apart. And with my lips open...

'Why don't you have a face-ectomy?' I said as I reached Mrs Gamble. 'Cowpat features like yours should carry a government health warning.'

Mrs Gamble, who I never said a bad word to before, fell back in total shock. Further shock rippled around the class. There was a little laugh over by the door, which opened all by itself, then closed, but I think I was the only one to notice, except maybe Angie. The demon genie had gone, which must mean I could go back to saying what I wanted instead of the stuff he put into my mouth.

I would start with a grovelling apology, and I didn't care who heard it.

'Miss,' I began.

'Yes!' she said coldly.

'Did anybody ever tell you that if you washed your armpits more than once a year you'd be a lot nicer to be around?'

'UUUUHHHH!' said the class.

'But I suppose where your folks come from, the steaming bogs of Planet Zod, deodorants haven't been invented yet.'

Mrs Gamble tried to say something else, but failed.

I tried not to say anything else, and also failed.

I told her she had hair like a second-hand toilet brush.

I asked her how her neighbours felt, living next door to a giant dung-beetle.

I suggested she start using *without delay* an ointment for people who have skin like a dead rhinoceros.

I told her to go and…

It was Angie who stopped me. She leapt out of her seat and threw herself at my legs, which gave way under me. When I was on the floor she jammed a knee into my throat, slapped masking tape across my mouth, then wound more tape round and round my head until the only part that wasn't taped was my eyes. Tutankhamen in a bobble hat. Stopped me talking though. Stopped me breathing too, until Angie drilled the blunt end of a pencil through the tape at the lower end of my nose. She did this twice, giving me a pair of fully functioning tape nostrils. Thinks of everything, that girl. But all this was too late to save me from Mrs Gamble's anger. I'd never seen her so mad. She ordered me into the corridor and told me to stay there. Before I went, Angie taped my wrists behind my back so I wouldn't be able to free my flapping trap.

Mrs Gamble gave a stern order to the class, then also came out. She couldn't look at me. I thought I might start bad-mouthing her through the masking tape, but it didn't happen. JR's spell, or whatever it was, must have run out of steam. Miss stalked off to the Head's office to arrange my lynching, while my classmates piled against the windows and stared at me. Some were pop-eyed with amazement.

Two or three boys raised clenched fists of support. I turned away. I no longer wanted to be a hero. I wanted to apologise to Mrs Gamble. I wanted her to like me again.

'You've really done it this time,' Angie said.

'Mm-umm-mm-um-er,' I said through the tape.

When Mrs G returned she still wouldn't look at me or speak to me. Mr Hubbard must have been back from the dentist's because she told Angie to escort me to his office. Angie led me away like a prisoner in a chain gang, except my chains were made of masking tape. When we were round the corner she yanked me to a halt and freed my wrists. When she unmasked my head I gulped oxygen.

'It wasn't me, Ange, it was him, JR! He took over my mouth!'

'I realise,' she said. 'But the things you *said* to her! The things you *called* her!'

'Don't remind me,' I wailed.

She left me to my misery outside Miss Prince's open door. Miss P stood wedged in a little alcove putting coffee granules and hot water into a mug. On the side of the mug was a scowling face, and the words: 'Who are you calling a mug?' Sad.

Like the mug, Miss Prince also scowled when she saw me. 'Wait,' she said sharply, proving that she'd heard the full story from Mrs Gamble. She took the coffee mug into the office and I heard her say something, heard a mumbled reply, then she came out again, minus mug. Still frowning, she held the door open for me. I went in. The door closed behind me. Mr Hubbard sat at his desk, hands folded in front of him. The dentist hadn't done him any favours. The left side of his jaw was twice its usual size. His lips on that side were all puffy and slack. He didn't invite me to sit down, so I just stood there, wondering if I should speak or what. He probably wanted to keep me guessing for a while, because the first thing he did was reach for the mug Miss Prince had brought in for him, and sip. The coffee poured straight out again, from the fat side of his mouth. It was so numb he didn't notice.

When he'd dribbled his fill, he spoke. 'Godbumbeepipert?' he asked sternly.

'Come again?' I said.

'Berpilgodlydinglebeeb?' Even more sternly.

'Er…Mrs Gamble said I have to report to you, sir.'

'Nippletodgerbuttfart,' he replied.

He sounded annoyed, so I decided to tell him the rest and hope he still understood English.

'Mr Hurley also told me to come and see you. And I did, but you weren't here.'

'Shlerpingumpyfinklegit?'

He was looking at my head.

'This little thing?' I touched the bobble with a finger.

'Ethflertitoff.'

'I can't take it off, sir. Like I told Mr Hurley, I have this chronic head disease which can only be caught by really bright kids and…and Heads. That means you. You wouldn't thank me if I took it off, sir.'

I knew he wasn't convinced by this when he jumped up from his seat and thumped the desk with a fist, shouting gibberish the while. Even if I couldn't understand him too well, I knew I was in trouble. I couldn't win, whatever I did. With this thought I came over all weary. Weary of having to make excuses, dream up new lies, wear a hat.

Specially the hat. I didn't *want* to wear it. Felt stupid in it. Besides, the wool was making my head hot. So I said:

'All right, I will then.'

I hauled the hat off. Mother Hubbard's eyes came out on springs.

'Blooooooomineck!' he said.

'Side effect of the contagious disease,' I told him.

'Ibbuh-ibbuh-ibbuh-ch-ch-choke?'

'Joke?' I said. 'Not for me it isn't.'

At this he gave a sort of roar, like someone who, once a year, at this very hour, turns into a slavering wild beast that wants to tear the living flesh off kids called McCue.

'Sir, calm down. It'll grow back. Maybe. And even if it doesn't I wouldn't be the first baldy in the world. There are bald actors, swimmers, doctors, teachers – look at Mr Prior. They probably get used to it once they've done the therapy.'

He still wasn't convinced. I could tell by all the unsubtitled shouting.

Suddenly the door bounced back and Miss Prince flew in. She must have been used to old Hubbard blowing his cool, because she leaned over his desk,

164

gripped him by the shoulders, and said: 'I've told you time and again not to see these brats, Hubert. You know they upset you.'

Mother Hubbard immediately stopped shouting and slumped in his chair. Miss Prince whirled on me, probably to tell me off for upsetting her boss. Except that she didn't. Her mouth moved, but nothing came out. She just stared. At my head. Which annoyed me. I was getting fed up of being stared at.

'Do you mind?' I said. 'It's only a head. You never seen a nude head before?'

She looked kind of puzzled at this, but still didn't say anything. Just raised her hand and pointed a trembling finger a bit above the top of my skull, which made me wonder if there was something else up there now, like a little genie satellite dish. I stepped into the outer office in search of a mirror. Found one on Miss Prince's desk, a very small one for looking at yourself in sections. I looked in, at section one, just above the eyebrows. Then I looked up a bit, next section. Then the next, and the next. I wasn't bald any more. Good news, you might think. But I didn't

have a full head of hair again. I had a full head of
something else instead.

Grass.

Very tall, very thick, very green grass.

With daisies.

Chapter Fifteen

I could hardly stay at school after that. I was right in it, go or stay, but at least no one would stare and point at my head at home. Till Dad came in anyway. I didn't even bother to put the hat on as I ran out of the school gates and along the street. After wearing a hat for half the morning it was good to feel the wind in my grass.

Reaching our road, I ran round the back of our house. Our back gate is about yo-high and bolted when we're out, so to get in I have to haul myself up, reach over the top, and pull the bolt back. I'd just done the hauling part and was about to pull the bolt when I heard a voice. JR's voice. I froze, half over the gate. Our back garden is sort of L-shaped, and his voice came from the part round the corner. I slid the bolt back very quietly, swung in on top of the gate, dropped down, and snuck up the path to the point where the fence turns. I looked round. There he was, JR, squatting in front of the kennel. He didn't look too happy. This was because Mad-Cat Stallone stood in the doorway, eyes luminous with rage, tail slapping his sides like a whip.

'You try my patience, Beast,' JR said fiercely. 'Leave my house this instant, I *command* thee!'

Stallone didn't seem impressed by the old-time language, or anything else about JR. He'd decided my dog kennel was going to be a cat kennel and no genie was going to tell him otherwise. His jaws reared apart, showing his sharp little teeth. In other words: 'Take a hike, bud.'

'I'll count to five,' JR said. 'If you're not on your way by then your paws won't touch the ground. Get it? Clear?'

The tone of voice probably did it for Stallone. No one speaks to him like that. He darted out of the kennel and sank his teeth in JR's arm. JR gave a shout of pain and jumped to his feet. Well, well, so genies can be hurt, I thought. There was blood on his arm too. Not human blood, more purple than red, but still blood. He muttered something that sounded awfully like a swear word, but in Mongolian, stepped back, and said, 'So! You defy

168

me!' in this super-deep voice with an echo. Then he pointed a finger at the family cat, and boomed: 'Begone, wretch!'

And Stallone bewent. Upward. I mean straight up, like a helicopter. When he reached roof level he spun round several times, as if trying to decide which way was north, and finally shot off over the houses, tail out behind him like the shaft of a firework rocket.

'And if I ever find you in my home again I'll turn you into a rug!' JR yelled after him. 'Hear me? A *rug!'*

I stepped out from hiding, applauding softly.

'Oh very good. Picking on poor defenceless animals now, are we, O Powerful One?'

JR turned. 'Shouldn't you be at school?'

'Of course I should be at school. But school isn't such a cool place for me right now, you saw to that.'

'Count yourself lucky I didn't turn you into a fly and drop you in a spider's web.'

'I'm supposed to be grateful for total baldness, then total grass, and being forced to call a teacher all the names under the sun?' Suddenly I felt really fed up about all this. 'It wouldn't be so bad if it wasn't just *me*,' I whined. 'No one else gets it in the neck, just good old fall guy McCue as per usual.'

Then I remembered that I wasn't the only one. I shielded my eyes. Stallone was just a dot in the blue distance now, still going strong. Would he ever come down, I wondered, or would he go into orbit and circle the Earth six times a day until he was just an angry assortment of flying fur and bones?

'Ah yes, your little gang,' JR said.

There was something in his voice that hauled my eyes back to earth in a hurry.

'My little...?'

'I'd forgotten. I was going to make them suffer too.'

I realised what I'd just put in his mind. Angie would murder me.

'I have a better idea,' I said. 'Let's shake hands and start again, all of us, you, me, Angie, Pete. You can live in my kennel rent free, and we...'

He wasn't listening. He was staring at the ground thinking of terrible things to do to the other two Musketeers. A nifty change of subject was called for.

'Mr Dent,' I said. He frowned, but still didn't pay

much attention. I tried again. 'Mr Dent? The Woodwork teacher who's really a genie?'

He looked up. I'd got him.

'Who *used* to be a genie,' he said.

'Used to be?'

'He no longer is.'

'Since when?'

'No idea. Years, possibly.'

'How do you know he's not one now?'

'When you look at another person, can you tell if he's human?'

'Well yeah, naturally. Oh, I see, you mean you can tell whether a person's a genie or an ex-genie just by looking at him.'

'Even without looking. I have very acute senses.'

'But why are you so afraid of a genie that isn't one any more?'

'It doesn't matter if he's a practising genie or a retired genie,' JR said. 'The Touch remains lethal.'

My pulse quickened. 'Touch? Lethal?'

He sighed, like all this conversation stuff was getting him down. But I had a feeling he was quite enjoying it. Must have been ages since he last talked about genie twaddle to a really intelligent person.

'Well, I don't suppose it matters if you know,' he said. 'It's very simple. If one genie is touched by another, even an ex-genie, by accident, the touched one is put out of action instantly and permanently.'

'Holy baloney. So if Mr Dent touched you...'

'I would lose almost all my powers and be trapped in this body for the rest of its ridiculously short life.'

'Bummer. Er...*almost* all your powers?'

'I'd be left with some small ability. All retired genies are. Nothing very useful or impressive. Nothing that would get people queuing for my autograph.'

'Would a retired genie like Mr Dent have a last small ability then?'

'Of course.'

'Like what?'

'You'd have to ask him. But I advise against it. If you let on that you know he's an ex-genie he might be alerted to my presence, and then I'd have to turn you into something tasty and feed you to something hungry.'

'Could he do, say, conjuring tricks?' I asked. I

didn't believe a word of this, but I had to keep his mind off Pete and Angie.

'Could who do conjuring tricks?'

'Mr Dent, now that he's an ex.'

'Possibly. Or perhaps he's good with wood. Very handy for someone passing himself off as a Woodwork teacher. Now if you'll excuse me, I have things to attend to.'

'What things?'

He grinned, and was suddenly a finger-clicking, gum-chewing, shoulder-rolling teenager again.

'Stick aroun', man.'

There was a puff of smoke. Then I was alone. And worried.

I reached into the garden gnome's backside for the door key. A small snail fell out of my grass. This stuff had to go, or birds and insects would start mistaking me for a wildlife haven and taking up residence. I went back round the L, broke open the dodgy padlock on the garden shed, and took out the shears. They were rusty and blunt, but cutting grass was what they were trained for. I sat down on the ground and got busy. Miss Prince's little mirror might have helped, but I didn't care how neat I looked. If I removed the daisies and snipped the grass really short I could tell Mum and Dad I'd dyed my hair green because green was all the rage. Dad would scoff, but Mum would try and be understanding. The good thing about being a kid is that when you do something really off the wall the Golden Oldies call it a 'phase'. You'd need six extra hands to count all the phases my parents think I've gone through.

Chapter Sixteen

As I hadn't planned to do a runner from school I'd left my bag there, in Mrs Gamble's class. My lunch was in my bag and it was almost lunchtime, so I had to find something else to eat. I toasted a couple of cheese and jam sandwiches, broke open a six-pack of Mars Bars, and watched one of my old videos. Must have been about three years old the last time I looked at this one. Happy days. Didn't know I was unlucky back then. Maybe I wasn't. Maybe the bad luck started later on. I settled back and watched the little cars tootling over perfect hillsides, the little clouds wandering across perfect skies, the little people having perfect little adventures, and for a while forgot my problems. When that video finished I put on another, different but just as perfect, and got into that, smiling sadly that life wasn't like that any—

BANG! BANG! BANG!

Rrring! Rrring! Rrriiiiiing!

I jumped with a squawk of alarm out of Perfect Little Video World.

BANG! BANG! BANG! BANG! BANG! BANG! BANG!

Rrring! Rrring! Rrring! Rrrrrrrrriiiiiiiiiiiiiiiiiiinn nnnnnggggging!

There was someone at the front door.

I was on my feet and almost in the hall before I remembered that I was off school without a licence. The Truancy Police had come for me! I returned to the TV and switched it off. I had to be quiet. So quiet they'd think the house was empty. What else do people do when they want to pretend they're not home? Of course! They turn the lights off! I flicked the switch. The light came on. Drat! It was broad daylight. I flicked it off again. Funnily enough I felt a bit safer with it off after it had been on. I looked about for somewhere to hide in case they kicked the door in anyway.

BANG-BANG-BANG-BANG-BANG-BANG-BANG!

Rrringringrrringrrringrrrrrrrrrriiiiiiiinnnnnngggg!

I jumped over the couch and scrunched down behind it. Maybe they wouldn't think to look there if they burst in, stun-guns blazing.

But then, in all the banging and ringing, I heard my name.

'Jig!'

'McCue!'

'Jiggyyyyy!'

I looked at the clock on the sideboard. What were Pete and Angie doing out of school so early? I climbed back over the couch and headed for the hall.

The banging was a bit less fierce by the time I reached the front door, as if the banger's fist was on its last legs. The ringing wasn't quite so hearty either, which probably meant that the battery was dying. I ripped the door back and stood aside. Pete and Angie shot in and landed in a tangled heap on the floor, along with three school bags, including mine, which they'd brought home for me.

'Why are you home so soon?' I asked, looking down at them.

They disentangled themselves and leapt to their feet. Pete thumped me on the shoulder. Then Angie thumped me on the other shoulder.

I staggered, rubbing my shoulders with opposite hands.

'What's that for, what have I done?'

'What you've *done*,' snarled Pete, 'is bring a genie into the world.'

'A genie that's really landed us in it,' said Ange.

'In...what?' I said, dreading the answer.

'The sort of ultra mess that brings Mother Hubbard round to see our parents,' said Pete.

I got nervous. 'When you say "our parents" you mean *your* parents – right?'

'I mean my dad, Angie's mum, your two.'

'We're supposed to tell them he'll be here around seven,' Angie said.

'Seven tonight?'

'No, seven the year after next,' said Pete. 'I'm gonna kill him!'

He pushed past me and rushed to the kitchen. Angie and I followed, more slowly.

'He seems a bit upset,' I said.

'He has good reason,' said Ange.

By the time we got to the kitchen Pete was out in the back garden, lying on the ground in front of the kennel. He knew about JR taking over the kennel, they both did. I'd told them at school about him making it bigger on the inside, furnishing it, hanging the Starving Artist pic on the wall.

'Come out here, you potty prawn!' Pete bawled into the kennel. 'I'm gonna sock you stupid! I'm gonna whack you to widdle! I'm gonna pulp you to porridge! I'm gonna—'

I closed the door to let him rant in peace. He was safe enough. He wouldn't have got beyond Threat One if JR had been in.

'What's this about?' I asked Angie. 'And why aren't you at school?'

'We were sent home. Half the school was. Because of what JR made Pete and me do.'

'Tell me.'

She told me. It had all started at lunchtime. They'd forgotten their packed lunches, so after they'd demolished mine they went to the dining hall. They were noshing with some of the other kids when Pete suddenly stood up and banged Ryan and Skinner's heads together.

'Good old Pete,' I said, impressed. But then I realised. 'Oh. Him.'

Angie nodded. 'Invisible. He appeared just long

enough to wave at me while Ryan was pushing Pete's face into someone's mash and gravy.'

'Pete likes mash and gravy,' I said.

'Not up his nose,' said Ange. 'Then I walked over to Mr Hubbard's table, and poured a jug of water over his head.'

'You poured a jug of water over the Head's *head*?'

'I didn't want to. Couldn't control myself.'

'So now you know what it's like.'

'But that was only the beginning. Some of the water must have got in Mother's mouth because he suddenly screwed his face up and spat out – all over Miss Prince, who jumped to her feet with a cry of: "Urine! This is urine!"'

'Very tasty, apparently,' I said.

'Everyone was still gaping and shouting,' Angie went on, 'when Pete and I grabbed hands and skipped out of the dining room.'

'You and Pete skipped out of the dining room?' I said. 'Holding *hands*?'

'I'll never live it down,' said a voice behind us. 'Pete Garrett holding hands and skipping! With a *girl!*'

Pete stood in the doorway. He looked more depressed than angry now.

180

'I still don't see why half the school was sent home,' I said.

'That was because of what we did next,' said Angie.

'Which was?'

'Run round the school putting the plugs in all the sinks and turning the taps full on. By the time they caught up with us half the building was under water.'

'Under pee,' said Pete. 'From the taps.'

'It was Mr Rice who nabbed us,' Angie said. 'Came splashing after us in his thumping great trainers, lifted us up by the collar like helpless little puddy tats, and hauled us before Mother.'

'He was back in his office by this time,' said Pete. 'Sitting on his blotter watching the piddle lap the legs of his desk.'

'From where he started to grill us,' Angie said.

'Like two rashers of streaky bacon,' said Pete.

'And what did we do while he lobbed questions at us?' said Angie.

'What?' I said.

'Laughed,' said Pete.

'Everything Hubbard said creased us up,' Angie

said. 'Even though it was about as funny as a baked sock. When we didn't stop – we couldn't – he went spare. Started screaming at us. Then Miss Prince ran in and started screaming too, but at him, telling him to calm down, watch his blood pressure, and all the time me and Pete went on cackling like hyenas on laughing gas.'

'So now you know why I want to kill your rotten genie,' said Pete.

'He's not my genie,' I said. 'Not now. I had him for about ten minutes, that's all, then I made him redundant.'

'If you hadn't peed in the Piddle Pool a thousand and one times he wouldn't be here, doing all this stuff. Maybe I ought to kill you instead.'

'Might not look too good on your school record.'

'I don't think I've got much to lose after today,' Pete said gloomily.

'After Mother Hubbard spills the beans to the Golden Oldies,' Angie said, 'we'll probably be on the dawn train to a juvenile detention centre in the Outer Hebrides.'

'Just us,' Pete said to me. 'You'll be able to wriggle out of it.'

A ray of hope. 'I will? How?'

'You just say you came over a bit weird in Mrs Gamble's class, apologise for cheeking her, and say the hat was just for a giggle.'

'Mr Hubbard and Miss Prince saw under the hat,' I said.

'So? You can buy bald wigs at the joke shop.'

'They didn't see me bald. They saw a full head of grass.'

They looked puzzled. I pointed to my head. They hadn't *noticed*???

'It's a pretty terrible haircut,' Angie said, 'but it's hardly grass.'

'What did you do,' Pete said, 'shove your nut in the food blender?'

I leaned down and checked my reflection in the door of the microwave. The grass wasn't grass any more. Must have turned back to hair while I was in Perfect Kiddie Vid Land. Great. Except that it looked as if it had been hacked about with blunt garden shears.

Chapter Seventeen

When they left, Pete was still trying to decide who he most wanted to murder, me or JR. Said he might return later with rat poison for one of us, or both. I was pretty bugged myself, but for different reasons. JR was unpredictable. All right, I'd got my hair back, but I had no idea if it was because he'd made it happen or if the grass spell had simply worn off. Point was, you never knew where you were with this genie. He certainly wasn't the sort you wanted for an enemy. Maybe I should try talking to him again. I went out to the garden, called softly.

'JR? JR, you around?'

If he was, he wasn't letting on. I dropped to my knees and looked in the kennel. It was pretty neat in there. Neat as in cool, neat as in neat. Even the bed was made. I was quite proud of my decorated and furnished kennel. Wouldn't have minded living there myself if the entrance had been bigger and there was a built-in toilet. You couldn't blame Stallone for wanting to move in. He'd never had a house of his own, just a basket and a litter tray.

'No hawkers,' a voice said. I looked up. 'No replacement window salesmen, no Bible thumpers, no lodgers, no humans.'

He looked normal for once. Too normal. His dreadlocks were pulled back and he wore polished black shoes, a silk tie, dark blue suit. He was even carrying a briefcase.

'You look like you're going for your first job interview,' I said, getting up.

'It's the new me,' he said.

'How long for?'

'Till the next new me. You ought to try it sometime, changing your image. That one does nothing for you.'

'I changed it today. Twice. Remember?'

He laughed. I didn't.

'Listen,' I said. 'What do you say to cutting us some slack? Letting us off the hook?'

'You'd like that, would you?' he said.

'Yes, I would actually.'

'OK.'

'What?' I said.

'I'll leave you alone.'

'You will? All three of us?'

'Sure. Long as you don't cross me. I'm bored with you three. There's a whole world out there, and I can do whatever I want with it. I'm going to have some fun.' He leaned towards me, grinning. 'Some *real* fun!'

'Oh now, wait,' I said. The world's in enough of a fix without you banging extra spokes in its wheels. Couldn't you amuse yourself some other way? Take up deep-sea fishing, potholing or something?'

He frowned. His briefcase turned into an enormous mallet.

'Perhaps I'll concentrate on you after all.'

'No, no,' I said, backing off. 'Do what you want. Go out and have yourself a ball at the world's expense.'

'Thanks. Your permission means so much to me.'

And with one puff of sarcastic smoke he was gone. Wish I could do that sometimes. Specially at school.

I went back in the house. Touch-and-go there for

a sec. But he'd said that we were out of the frame so long as we didn't upset him. Shame about the rest of the world, but at least the Musketeer corner could breathe again. I went up to my room, threw my school clothes on the floor, changed into civvies. Then I got on my bed and lay there with my hands under my head listening to music and thinking what a boring ceiling I had. In a while my eyelids got heavy. I nodded off.

And had yet another maggoty nightmare.*

I was sitting at a table, and there was this huge crusty pie in front of me. I don't know what sort of pie, but it looked really terrific, really, you know…edible. While I was smacking my dreamy lips in anticipation, the pie split apart, and I saw what was inside. Maggots. Thousands and thousands of live maggots. I wanted to kick my chair back and run from the table, but the only part of me that could move was one of my arms, and the hand on the end of it that reached out with a spoon and scooped pie. Then, heaving with maggots, the spoon headed for my mouth. I could almost taste the horrible little beasts. Any second and I *was* going to taste them. Closer and closer,

---

* Can you have a nightmare in the middle of the day? Day is the opposite of night, and the opposite of mare is horse. So maybe a bad dream that's not at night should be called a dayhorse. But I'll stick with nightmare. Mainly because 'having a dayhorse' sounds so stupid.

the spoon came. It reached my mouth. Wriggly little bodies crawled onto my lips. My mouth opened, and—

Pitter-patter-putt.

Yes, *pitter-patter-putt*. That's the sound that saved me from eating the maggot pie in my nightmare. Have you ever noticed in films and TV dramas how nightmares usually end with the dreamer jerking into a sitting position covered in sweat? I've never done that. Probably no one has in real life. I usually wake up with my head under the pillow.

Pitter-patter-putt.

My eyelids jumped back. My music had finished and the room was quiet, apart from the sharp little pattering sound. I lifted my head to see where it was coming from. Tiny little stones were hitting the closed window, on the outside. Odd, I thought. Why would stones be hitting my window? I might have lain there wondering about this for some time if another stone – a bigger one, about the size of a fist – hadn't hit the glass. Because it was bigger than the others, this one didn't just patter and fall neatly away on the other side. It shattered the window. It came into the room. And once inside it didn't just drop to the carpet with a satisfied sigh, as if to say, 'My work is done'. No. It whizzed further in, towards the bed. And landed. On me. And where exactly do you think it landed? On my shoulder? My chest? One of my knees? Any of these would have been bad enough, but the stone had other plans. It wanted to land on the very last place a boy who isn't wearing a cast-iron codpiece wants a fist-sized stone to land. And it did.

I yeeked. I bucked. I rolled off the bed on to my knees and elbows, and just hung there for a while, cradling my whatnots, until it occurred to me that if one stone could hit the bull's-eye, another might come after it in search of another bull's-eye. I struggled to my feet. I hobbled to the wall beside the window. No more fist-sized stones leapt up at the glass. Even the small ones had stopped. I twitched the edge of the curtain and peeked out. Angie was down in the garden, looking up. I trod broken glass and opened what was left of the window.

'What do you think you're doing?!' I yelled.

'Wasn't me,' she said. 'I was happy with small

pebbles, but you know Pete.'

'Where is the little twonk?' I growled.

Angie said something to the corner of the house and Pete joined her.

'Sorry, Jig.'

'Sorry? *Sorry?!* What do I tell Mum and Dad about this window?'

'Say it was a vandal.'

'It was a vandal. You.'

'We were trying to attract your attention,' Angie said.

'You succeeded.'

'We knocked on the door first,' Pete said. 'You didn't answer.'

'I didn't hear. What is it this time?'

'Come down and we'll tell you,' said Angie.

'Tell me from there.'

'I said come *down*! Now! Front door, thirty seconds!'

She charged round the side of the house to tap her foot impatiently on the step till I got there. I sighed. The Mint had spoken. I was about to step back from the shattered window to do as I'd been told when I saw Pete aim a kick at the kennel.

'Oi!' I yelled. 'That's my Woodwork project!'

'It's where *he* holes up,' he snarled up at me.

'Still. How would you like it if I kicked your stupid ashtray?'

I left the window (mostly on the floor) and hobbled out of my room. Went downstairs sideways, one hand on the rail, the other hoisting the Tommy Rollocks. Pete started thumping the door even before I reached it.

'Will you stop banging this *door*!' I yelled, tearing it open. They didn't fall in this time.

'You look rough,' Angie said.

'So would you if your personal equipment had just been stoned to death. What's this all about?'

'Neil Downey phoned.'

'Downey phoned? You broke my window to tell me that *Downey* phoned?'

'He wanted to remind us to go to his party tonight.'

'Remind us to…?'

I'd forgotten about Downey's party. And it could stay forgotten. I had more important things to think about. At least two.

'Downey's party's just what we need,' said Pete.

'It's the last thing I need,' I said, throbbing quietly.

'Oh, you'd rather hang around here, would you, listening to Mother Hubbard trash you to your parents while you shuffle your feet and twist your hands behind your back?'

'I can wriggle out of that, you said so yourself.'

'I lied. Hubbard is so hopping, there'll be Musketeer blood sloshing along *both* sides of the street by the time he's done.'

'Maybe so, but do you seriously think the Golden Oldies will let us go to a party when we tell them the Head's coming over to discuss plans for a triple crucifixion?'

Angie rapped her knuckles on my forehead like it was another door.

'Hello? Anybody home?'

'Don't *do* that!' I said, jerking back.

'We don't tell the GOs he's *coming*,' she said. 'We nip off to Downey's before Mother *gets* here. Geddit? Sinking in?'

'You're forgetting something. We have the kind of folks that don't let us cross the road without a signed note. When we go to parties they want to meet the parents, the grandparents, and the skeleton in the closet.'

'Ours'll let us go this time, no worries,' Pete said.

'Why, what's so different this time?'

'We're going to make our beds and tidy the house,' said Angie.

'Duh?' My mind wasn't on this. It was several tads lower down.

'When Dad and Audrey find that we've done stuff without being bribed or threatened,' Pete said, 'they'll be so fazed they'll say yes to anything. Works every time. You ought to try it.'

'If you're coming be ready by half six,' said Angie. 'If not, see you when the grounding ends in two thousand and forty-three.'

They went. I closed the door and leaned on it for a minute before doing a Hunchback of Notre Dame to the kitchen. The blast of icy air when I opened the freezer was so refreshing that I was tempted to drop my pants and cool off where it counted. The reason I didn't was that I knew this would be a signal for some total stranger to paste his eyes to the window. I rummaged in the freezer for something to give Mum and Dad for tea. Best way to Golden Oldie hearts is through their stomachs, I always find. Ah! Mediterranean Four Fish Pizza with Green Olives! Perfect. Not only would Mum appreciate me putting junk like that in front of her, but I could avoid the 'spoilt brat' row when I refused to eat it some other time.

I turned the pizza box over and started the big search for cooking instructions in English. Even when I found them the bit about getting the wrapper off was so complicated that my mind wandered. It didn't wander far, just a few minutes back, to my latest nightmare. Maggot pie – ugh! Made me feel sick just to think about it. What was it with maggots all of a sudden? I'd never dreamed of them till Downey brought that tin of them to school, and suddenly every time I drop off my head's crawling with them. Still, I thought, a person can't keep on dreaming about the same things. With any luck I'd seen the last of them now.

With any *luck*? Who was I kidding? That's what had started all this. Luck, lack of. I didn't know it, but I hadn't seen anything yet!

Chapter Eighteen

My mother and father have this equal-share system about the evening meal. Mum prepares it and Dad sits in front of the TV till it's ready. I hadn't told him there'd be a different chef tonight, but he probably wouldn't have cared. While he watched sporty types do stuff with balls, I shoved the pizza in the oven, laid the table, and practised the Really Helpful Son expression for when Mum came home. As it happened I didn't need this because by the time she eventually got in I'd had to whip the pizza out three times to stop it becoming a ceramic.

'Where have you been?' I shouted. 'I've had your tea ready for ages and you don't even have the decency to let me know you're coming home *late*!'

This threw her. She took in the laid table, the blue paper napkins, the knives and forks, the bottle of supermarket wine Dad won in a raffle a while back.

'You've made the tea? *You've* made the *tea*?'

I switched on the Very Hurt look.

'I thought it'd be nice for you to come home and find it ready for a change. Just you and Dad, all cosy, seeing as I'm not here tonight.'

'What do you mean not here tonight?'

I slapped my head with exasperation.

'I *told* you! Neil Downey's *birthday* party! I'd be on my way by now if you'd come home at a reasonable time!'

'Neil Downey's birthday party? First I've heard about it. First I've heard of a Neil Downey, come to that.'

'Kid in our class. I told you two weeks ago about the party.'

'Did you?'

I hadn't, of course, but when you tell mothers that you already told them something they think they haven't remembered because at their age their memory is only fit for scrap.

'Yes. I did.'

I headed for the front door. Opened it.

'Jiggy!'

I stopped, eyeing the street, which I was keen to get into.

'Yes?'

'What's happened to your hair?'

'I blame global warming,' I said, and shut the door on her.

When I rang Pete and Angie's bell the door was opened by Angie's mum, Audrey. She wore the same dazed expression I'd just seen on my mother's face across the road.

'This is where I say you look like you've seen a ghost,' I said.

'Almost as shocking,' she said. 'Angie and Pete have tidied the house!'

'Stop their pocket money, that's my advice. Are they ready?'

She yelled up the stairs – 'Angie! Pete! Jiggy's here!' – then turned back to me. 'They told me ages ago about this party you're going to, Angie says. I don't remember. Forgetting everything these days.'

'Next stop the Really Ancient People's Home,' I said.

'Think I'll make the booking right away before I forget,' she said, and wandered into the kitchen.

Angie rattled down the stairs. She looked really

neat: green top, white jeans, good shoes, hair all tidy.

'Aren't you coming?' she said.

'Yes. Seemed a good idea.'

'But you're dressed like a tramp.'

'I'm dressed like I always dress.'

'Exactly. Jig, we're going to a party.'

'Only Downey's.'

'It doesn't matter whose, you're supposed to dress up for parties.' She turned to the stairs. 'PETE! GET A MOVE ON!'

Pete came down. Slowly, dragging his feet like he wanted to leave them behind.

'All that's missing is the halo,' I said.

'Don't start,' he said.

Angie must have stood over him with a whip, because there's nothing else would make him put on a freshly ironed shirt, pressed jeans, polished shoes, and smarm his hair down. Angie yelled goodbye to the house and slammed the door.

'Where does Downey live anyway?' I asked as we headed off.

'Other side of the old brickworks,' Ange said.

'How do you know?'

'I drew a map on the phone.'

'Paper would have been better,' said Pete.

'We ought to keep away from the roads in case Hubbard's early,' I said.

'Cut through the park?' said Angie.

'Yeah.'

First thing I noticed when we entered the park was that the Starving Artists' tent was gone. I might have mentioned this if Angie hadn't halted suddenly, and said:

'You know what we forgot, don't you? A present for Downey.'

'We're going to his rotten party, isn't that enough?' Pete said.

'You can't go to someone's party without a present,' Angie said. 'We have to take *something*.'

We looked about us. Trees, bushes, flowers, birds, dog mess.

'Spoilt for choice,' I said.

'Hey, I know,' said Pete, and spun round, headed back towards the gates.

'Where you going?'

'To get a present for Downey.'

'What present?'

'Wait and see.'

'You're not going back to the estate?'

'That's where it is.'

'But we left in a hurry in case Mother H showed up early.'

'He'll never recognise me out of school,' Pete said, walking backwards. 'Specially looking like this. Even I had trouble when I looked in the mirror.'

'Wonder what he's got in mind?' Angie said when he'd gone.

'Knowing Pete...' I ticked off the possibilities. 'One of his old whoopee cushions, black face soap, itching powder, his collection of one-legged foot soldiers from the Crimea...'

Just ahead of us on the path there was a big waste bin overflowing with fish and chip wrappers. Beside the bin was a bench covered in pigeon droppings. As we made for the bench to wait for Pete, something caught my eye up above.

'Look at *that*, Ange!'

Angie looked up. 'Wow.'

Lions, giraffes, zebras, rhinos, every kind of animal you can think of, were floating across the sky.

'Amazing what they can do with balloons these days,' I said.

'Yeah, they look so *real*. The hippo's legs are actually moving!'

We fell on to the bench, leaned back, gazed up at the sky.

'And look at the giraffe,' I said. 'That neck! Work of art!'

Most of the giant balloon-animals were moving one part or another – legs, tail, head, ears. Even the *eyes* moved!

'Must be a Zoo stunt to get more visitors,' Angie said.

'If this doesn't work nothing will. Never saw anything like it.'

We were smiling appreciatively up at the fantastic sky show when something even more lifelike happened. The rhino balloon, which was almost exactly overhead, dropped something. Something dark, which grew bigger and bigger and bigger, until –

KER-PLOPP!

– it landed on the path less than a million light years from our feet and spattered everything within spatter distance. Angie looked at her white jeans, which now had an interesting brown speckled pattern.

'Jig,' she said, in hushed tones.

'Yes?' I replied, also hushed.

'I don't think they're balloons.'

'I think you're right. This doesn't look too good.'

'Nor do my jeans. You know what this means, don't you?'

'Trip to the dry cleaners?'

'Means he's moved on to bigger things.'

'When you say "he"...?'

'Who else could make very big wingless animals fly?'

'I should have expected something like this,' I said.

'Why's that?'

'He told me he was bored with us three. Said it's a big world and he was going to have some fun with it. Looks like the fun's started.'

Chapter Nineteen

We hadn't moved. Didn't seem much point. The flying animals were minding their own business, and we were minding the rhino's. The enormous whoopsie from space steamed contentedly in the sun near our feet. It did not smell like a bed of roses.

'I think we ought to put our heads together over this,' Angie said.

'Yeah, that should clear the sinuses.'

'And come up with some plan for getting rid of that pest.'

'He's an all-powerful genie, Ange. We're all-non-powerful mortals. Sort of unequal contest.'

'There has to be a way.'

I sighed. 'Pity about Mr Dent.'

'Mr Dent?'

'I mean it's a pity he's not an ex-genie, like JR thinks he is. If he really was an ex-genie, he could zap JR's powers with a single touch.'

'What do you mean, *ex*-genie?'

'He's retired, JR says.'

'And "zap his powers with a single touch"?'

I brought her up to speed on the Genie Touch.

'Yeah, but even if he was an ex-genie,' Angie said, 'he wouldn't necessarily help us against one of his own.'

'Course he would, he's one of our teachers.'

'You're smiling. What am I missing?'

'I was just imagining Mr Dent curled up in an old lamp or bottle.'

'He'd have to be quite a bit smaller than he is now.'

'As a genie he could make himself any size he wanted, no sweat.'

'It would explain the head dent,' Angie said.

'What would?'

'Well if he used to live in a bottle, and the bottle had a stopper of some sort that pressed down on his head, after a few decades or so there'd have to be a dent, wouldn't there?'

Her gaze returned to her jeans and she came over all thoughtful. My jeans were just as spattered, but they hadn't started out white, so I didn't get

204

thoughtful. I looked up to see how the flying zoo was doing. JR must be killing himself, running a show like that, I thought. The animals were turning slowly round and round, bumping into one another, bouncing off.

'Remember when we found JR hiding in Rubbish Bin Corner?' Angie said. 'We asked how he knew Mr Dent was a genie and he touched his head. We thought he was saying that he just knew, but maybe he was saying "by the dent in his head – the stopper mark".'

I unplugged my eyes from the roof display.

'If genies have to have stopper marks, why hasn't JR got one?'

'Never lived in a bottle. No stoppers in Piddle Pools.'

'Woh,' I said.

'Woh what?'

'I just remembered something that happened when me and Mr D were shovelling sawdust into little sacks.'

'When you were…?'

I told her how I'd bumped into Mr Dent after I failed to see Mother Hubbard the first time; how

I gave him a hand in the old Woodwork shop. Then I told her what I'd just remembered.

'Before he was a Woodwork teacher Mr Dent had some sort of magic act.'

'Magic act?'

'That's what he said. He did a trick to prove it.'

I told her about the egg with the little beak inside.

'Not exactly genie league stuff,' Angie said.

'No, but maybe it's all he can do if he's retired. Could be that when JR first saw him it wasn't just the stopper mark that told him Dent had genie blood. Maybe he sensed Mr D's last little bit of magic.'

'Hmm,' said Angie. She wasn't convinced.

'And there's more,' I said. 'Mr Dent told me that between giving up the "magic" and becoming a Woodwork teacher he sold carpets. Turkish carpets. *Flying* carpets.'

'He told you that?'

'Dropped a pretty hefty hint. Said they flew out of the shop when he was there. Genies and flying carpets...sort of go together, don't they?'

'Mm-mm.' She still looked doubtful.

'But that's not all,' I said, really on the case now. 'You know JR has purple eyes?'

'Yes, so?'

'Well when I first met him he told me that all genies have purple eyes, and whatever they turn themselves into, if it has eyes, those eyes are purple.'

'Mr Dent doesn't have purple eyes. He has very blue eyes. After the dent in his forehead his eyes are what you most notice about him.'

'He wears contact lenses.'

'He doesn't!'

'Does.'

'How do you know?'

'One of them fell out while we were trowelling sawdust.'

'Wow. So…his eyes aren't blue?'

'I didn't see. But they could be any colour. Even purple.'

'Jig, are you saying that Mr Dent really is a retired genie?'

'Nah. Course not.'

I laughed. She joined in. We stopped at the same moment.

'Amazing how much evidence points to him

being one though,' Angie said.

'Yes. Amazing amount.'

'Mr Dent, an ex-genie. Do you realise how *insane* that sounds?'

'Any more insane than flying giraffes and hippos?'

She looked up. ''Bout equal, I'd say.'

And in that instant we knew, beyond any shadow of a doubt, that Mr Dent, Woodwork teacher, really was a retired genie.

'How about those balloons? So real!' It was Pete, returning. He took in the steaming mound on the path, wrinkled his nose. 'Must have been a heck of a dog,' he said.

Then I saw the thing he'd gone back for. I stared in disbelief. Something fat and slimy rose in my throat. My stomach lurched.

'How did you get this?'

'I rang your front door bell, told your mum that you'd sent me back for something you left in the garden, she said "Help yourself", I went out and hooked it off the kennel wall with her clothes prop, and zipped out the back gate so she wouldn't see it. Smart, eh?'

'It's not *that* smart,' I said, averting my eyes from the Starving Artist painting.

'What do you mean?'

'What he *means*,' said Angie, 'is that JR might be kind of miffed that someone's swiped something he likes enough to put on his wall.'

Pete grinned. 'That's the beauty of it. Not only do we have a free gift for Downey but we get back at that pond life for what he did to us today. It's not half what he deserves, but it's better than nothing.'

'Pete,' I said. 'I've done a deal with JR. He said he'll leave us alone so long as we don't upset him. Do you think he's going to just let it go when he discovers that one of us has nicked his picture?'

Pete's grin dipped a little. 'He won't know it was me. Will he?'

'I think he can find out anything he wants to. And I think he'll hare after the nicker with a pitchfork and pitch it where forks aren't meant to go.'

He sat down with a thump on the bench.

'I risked life and limb to get this.'

'You only asked my mother.'

209

'Not your mother, Stallone. He almost turned me to cat meat when I lugged the picture out.'

'Stallone was there?' I said.

'In the kennel. I never saw him so wild.'

'So he's come back…'

'Didn't know he was ever away.'

'He sort of flew off earlier.'

'It does solve our problem, though,' Angie said.

I looked at her. 'What solves which problem?'

'The picture. The present for Downey. We've got nothing else.'

'That's right,' said Pete. 'So let's get to Downey's and give it to him before Mr Hey-Riddle-Piddle misses it. Once Downey has it JR might think it was him that took it, and shred him instead of me.'

'Many happy returns, Neil,' I said.

'No wrapping paper,' Angie said.

'There's loads,' Pete said, tugging fish and chip wrappers out of the waste bin.

'We can't use that,' I said. 'Smells of fish.'

'Downey smells worse, probably won't notice.'

Angie smoothed out a couple of fishy wrappers and folded them round the picture. My stomach whistled with relief once it was covered. We didn't have any sticky tape, but Ange tucked the corners in as well as she could.

'Pen anyone?' she said when this was done.

I handed over my felt-tip. She wrote on the greasy giftwrap.

HAPPY BIRTHDAY NIEL
FROM PETE, JIGGY AND ANGIE

'Not like you to put yourself last,' Pete said to her.

'Yes, well, I'm not proud of this.'

'I wouldn't be either,' I said. 'Neil is "ei".'

'Is it? Oh well, Downey can't spell.'

'He's probably got the hang of his own name by now.'

Angie slapped the fish-wrapped Starving Artist painting against Pete's chest. We carried on across the park.

Chapter Twenty

By the time we reached the opposite park gates, Pete had cottoned on to the fact that the flying animals weren't life-size balloons. And he was worried. If JR could do big stuff like that, what would he do to a person who stole from him? He tried dumping Downey's present in a waste bin, but Angie told him that if he didn't take it out she'd stick him in there with it. He wailed a bit, but hauled the thing out, then knotted his snotty handkerchief round the bottom half of his face as a disguise.

There were plenty of vehicles in the street on the other side of the park, but none were moving. Drivers and passengers, along with every pedestrian, were staring up at the sky, where all but one of the animals were flying into the distance. The one that wasn't going anywhere was an elephant, which was zigzagging around like one of those planes that writes vapour messages. Very like one actually, because smoke was coming out of its rear jet – and turning into a message.

Unlike everyone else we didn't wait to see the rest of the show. We soon reached the site of the old brickworks. The filling in of the Piddle Pool had already started. There was all this buildery stuff round it – mechanical digger, truck full of rubble, pickaxe, Portaloo. No workmen. Across the rocky ground we stumbled. Beyond was open country. Very flat country. The earth was almost black out there, with nothing growing anywhere apart from a handful of sickly-looking trees. It was all so depressing that you wouldn't have been a bit surprised if the big black birds flapping slowly overhead had suddenly decided that now would be an excellent time for a mass suicide and plunged to Earth, beak first.

'Little on the gloomy side,' I said.

'Little on the-end-of-the-world side,' said Pete through his hanky, which now had a wet mouth-shape in it.

We came to a stony old track that couldn't possibly have led anywhere but the Twilight Zone.

'This is it,' said Ange.

'This is what?' I said.

'Downey's road.'

'How can you tell?' said Pete.

'The sign, dummy.'

'Sign? What sign?'

'Are you *blind*?' she said, slamming a party shoe down on a small stone at our feet. We dropped our eyes to small stone level and read what was painted on it in shaky white capitals.

'What is it,' I said, 'some sort of code?'

'No it's not code, it's an abbreviation.'

'Why is it abbreviated?'

'Probably because the stone isn't big enough to write it in full.'

'So why didn't the morons get a bigger stone?' Pete said.

'How the hell would I know?' said Angie.

214

'What does the abbreviation stand for?' I asked.

She held the scrap of paper with Downey's address two centimetres from my eyes, which made them cross.

I removed my cross eyes from the paper and aimed them along the track, at a distant house.

'That must be Downey's then.'

'Not necessarily,' Angie said.

'But it's the only house.'

'He told me Number Two, Sink Hole Drove. "Number Two" kind of gives the impression that there's also a Number One, probably before it.'

She walked into the dead field to our left and peered into the distance under her hand.

'Yes, another house. Between that one and some big grey ugly building.'

We were about to continue on our way when

Pete took a flying kick at the Sink Hole Drove stone.

'Just in case it's that genie in disguise,' he said as it bounced away.

We waited till we were sure the stone wasn't going to do anything unstoneish, then set off along the track.

'Why do the French only eat one egg for breakfast?' Pete asked seconds later.

'I didn't know they did,' I said.

'It's a joke. Why do the French only eat one egg for breakfast?'

I sighed. 'I don't know, Pete, why do the French only eat one egg for breakfast?'

'Because to a French person one egg is an *oeuf*.'

Angie and I looked at the sky for help. There wasn't any. Only an elephant writing a smoky message with its backside.

THE JIMMY RIDD

'He's spelling out his name,' Angie said.

'The elephant's called Jimmy Ridd?' said Pete.

'He's so full of himself now,' I said, meaning JR,

not Pete or the elephant, 'that he's probably forgotten about Mr Dent.'

'What's Mr Dent got to do with anything?' Pete again.

'JR thinks he's a genie.'

'JR is a genie.'

'I'm talking about Mr Dent.'

'What about him?'

'JR thinks he's a genie.'

'Oh yeah.'

'Ex-genie,' said Angie.

'Right,' I said.

'Ex-genie?' said Pete.

'No longer is,' said Angie.

'Since when?' said Pete.

'Who knows?' I said.

'Looks as if he's right too,' said Angie.

'Who?' said Pete.

'JR,' said Angie.

'Right about what?'

'About Mr Dent being an ex-genie.'

'How'd you work that out?'

'Long story,' said Angie.

'Tell me,' said Pete.

'No point, you wouldn't believe it.'

'Try me.'

'Do you want to explain or shall I?' Angie said to me.

'Go ahead,' I said.

She took a deep breath, gave him all the facts, all the evidence. And when she'd finished...

'You're right, I don't believe it,' Pete said.

We walked on.

'Some Drove,' I said as we drew near the first of the two houses.

'Huh?' said Angie.

'Sink Hole Drove, but no drivers, or even drovers. No cars.'

'It's not exactly a major highway.'

'No, but there's a party up ahead. Parties have guests. Some guests are driven. By car. So where are the cars?'

'Maybe there aren't any other guests,' said Pete. 'Maybe we're the only ones and they're going to slit our throats and hang us from one of the dead trees for the birds to peck our flesh off.'

As we got closer the track curved a bit, so we could see the second house and the big grey ugly building at the back of it. Both houses were very ordinary, covered in brown pebbledash, with little iron gates at the front. The first gate had the number '1' on it. We looked over it as we passed – and stopped.

'What a garden!' Angie said.

It was too. I never saw so many flowers in one eyeful. Huge, some of them, brilliant colours, petals like snow shoes. And in the middle of that gloomy landscape too, where nothing else grew.

'Well look who it isn't,' said Pete.

Some way into the flowery garden, in a semicircle of giant sunflowers, a tall thin man sprawled in a deckchair. He wore a flowery shirt, blue shorts, and dark glasses on top of his head.* It was Mr Flowerdew, our Science teacher. Serious, black-suited Mr Flowerdew in shorts and summery shirt, dozing in a deckchair.

'Downey kept this quiet,' Angie said.

'A teacher next door,' said Pete. 'I wouldn't like that. I'd never want to turn my music up or yell at my dad or go out with my hair uncombed.'

Even dozing, Mr Flowerdew must have heard his name, or our voices, because he dropped his shades

---

* No, no, only the *glasses* were on his head!

over his eyes and turned to see who was gawping over his gate.

'Move it!' I said. 'One thing we don't need is polite chats with off-duty teachers.'

'Too late,' said Angie.

He was already half out of his deckchair, so we froze to give him a chance to reach us. He took some getting used to, in his fancy open-necked shirt, knobbly knees to the world. Even dressed like that, soaking up the sun, he didn't look too well.

'What are you three doing all the way out here?'

'Going to Neil Downey's birthday party,' I replied.

'I didn't know it was Neil's birthday.'

'It isn't,' said Pete through his hanky.

'Who are you meant to be?' Sir said to him.

'Who are you?' Pete said, but he took the hanky off.

'This your place, sir?' Angie asked.

'It is, yes.'

'Nice garden.'

'Well, thank you.'

She said something else complimentary and Mr Flowerdew looked pleased in his sickly way, and right away they were having a real old jaw about flowers. Angie has just about zero interest in flowers, but you'd never guess to hear her and Flowerdew yammering about them.

'Jig.' Pete nudged me in the ribs.

He was looking up at the sky. I did likewise. The jet-elephant's smoky message was complete. It said:

THE JIMMY RIDDLE SKYSHOW

'Stupid genie,' Pete muttered.

Mr Flowerdew must have heard this, because he broke off in the middle of a flowery sentence and also looked up. When he saw, his shades almost popped off in amazement. He'd missed the best bit, the elephant writing the message with its jacksie, but he couldn't miss it zooming off after the other animals now that it had finished.

'Did you say…genie?' Mr Flowerdew said, in a small tight voice.

'Pete's little joke,' I said. 'Real joker, Pete.'

'We'd better go, we'll be late,' Angie said, and

shooed Pete and me ahead of her like cattle. 'Bye, sir.'

He didn't answer. Hadn't heard. Couldn't take his eyes off the sky.

We were still some way short of Number Two, Sink Hole Drove, when we noticed the smell. A real stink, like something that had died months ago and been left out in the sun.

'Kind of like the smell Downey carries round with him,' Pete said.

'Which means it's not him, but where he lives,' I said. 'Must cling to his clothes.'

'Which means it'll cling to ours,' said Angie. She looked down at her rhino-spattered jeans. 'Not that it matters *now*.'

Chapter Twenty-one

Even without the smell you could tell which was the party house. A wrinkled balloon drooped from the gate. Our spirits wrinkled with it.

'Maybe we can make our excuses after the first wobbly jelly and shoot off home,' I said.

'You forget,' Angie said. 'Home is not where we want to be right now. We're here to get *away* from home.'

We pushed the little iron gate back. Walked up the path. Downey's front garden wasn't a patch on Mr Flowerdew's. The grass was all brown and withered, like it hadn't rained here all year, and you could count the number of flowers without needing to know double figures. It was a fairly neat garden, though. Looked like someone had done their best with it. The windows were clean, too, and the window frames and front door had been painted quite recently. But the smell! It got worse and worse the closer we got to the house. Just before we reached the door, which was open, a woman appeared in it. Smallish woman, tidy like the garden, with a big smile. She held her hands out to us.

'You must be Angie, Pete and Jiggy. I'm Edina Downey.'

'Downey's mum?' Angie said in surprise as her hands were taken.

She was surprised because Mrs Downey seemed nice. Stinkpot Downey and a nice mother didn't fit somehow. Pete and I hung back. We don't encourage total strangers to hold our hands, nice or not.

Then Downey himself was there, and his mother dropped Angie's hands and went inside. He was all dressed up in a smart blue shirt, grey trousers, spray-on hair like Pete's. I was starting to feel like I should use the tradesman's entrance.

'You came!' he cried, and for a second I thought he was going to hug us. Hairs rose on the back of my neck.

'Course we did, Neil,' Angie said. 'Wouldn't miss your late birthday party for anything.'

'Cool jeans, Ange,' Downey said. Sad thing was, he meant it.

We were just going in when the day went dark and there was a mighty overhead rumble. A black cloud had rolled over the sun. Angie and I exchanged nervous glances.

'Probably nothing,' she said.

'Nah. Freak weather thing.'

But I had experience of freak weather things, and was the first to shoot past Downey into the house. Angie didn't hang about either. Nor Pete.

Mrs Downey turned out to be just one of the surprises in this household. Downey also had a younger brother and sister. The boy was about eight, the girl four or five. They were dressed up too, and also seemed happy to see us.

'Neil's dad is out back tending to the stock,' Mrs Downey said. 'He'll be with us shortly.' She showed us into a room with a long table covered with party tea stuff, balloons hanging from the ceiling, two birthday cards on a little side table.

'Forgot to bring a card,' I whispered.

'So did everyone else,' Angie whispered back.

'There isn't anyone else,' whispered Pete. 'I told you, we're it.'

Downey caught Pete's whisper, probably because

you can usually hear Pete's whispers in the next room.

'You're the first to arrive,' he said.

'Really?' I said. 'I thought we were late.'

'You are.'

'People often have trouble finding us out here,' Mrs Downey said. 'None of Neil's friends from school have made it yet.'

All this time the little Downey kids were standing looking up at us. The little Downey girl was holding Angie's hand and the little Downey boy had a finger up his nose.

'The entertainment should be here soon,' Downey said. 'Special late birthday treat.'

'Um, Neil...' Angie said. I knew that she felt kind of obliged to switch to 'Neil' from 'Downey' in front of his mother. 'We've got something for you.'

'Something for me?'

His eyes almost drowned with gratitude as she yanked the greasy package from under Pete's arm.

'It's from all of us,' she said, handing him the package.

'Oh Neil, a *present*, isn't that *nice*?' Mrs Downey said.

Neither of them said anything about the state of the wrapping or the wrong spelling of his name, they just seemed thrilled that we'd brought him something. The paper fell to the floor. When Downey saw what was inside his grateful smile also fell.

'Is this a joke?' he said to Pete. Everyone knows about Pete's lousy jokes.

'Ask the artist,' said Pete.

'Where'd you get it?'

'An exhibition,' Angie said. 'Don't you like it?'

Even Mrs Downey's smile had gone a bit tight. 'They weren't to know, darling. It's a lovely thought.' She looked at us. 'It's just that we already have a few of these.'

'Paintings?' I said.

She nodded.

'Yeah, but not like this,' said Pete. 'Can't be many around like *this*.'

'You'd be surprised,' said Downey.

It was a relief when the embarrassing conversation was interrupted by one of those comic motor horns that my dad says should be banned. Mrs Downey rushed to a window.

'It's the entertainer! I'll go and welcome him. He'll have some things to set up, I expect.'

'At least someone else bothered to come,' I said quietly.

'Only 'cos they're paying him,' said Pete.

'I'll show you our paintings,' said Downey

He left the room carrying our present. We followed him. The little sister came too, still gripping Angie's hand, but the kid brother stayed put, gazing at the table with hungry eyes and sucking the finger from his nose. Downey led the way down the hall. The house was neat and clean, but everywhere you went there was this horrible smell that he carried to school with him.

'Maybe it's a new kind of fresh air spray,' Angie whispered. 'Like Lavender or Spring Bouquet.'

'Yes,' I whispered back. 'Rotting Flesh could really catch on.'

The room he took us to didn't have a carpet, just black floorboards spattered with paint. The only furniture was a wooden kitchen chair, a big black easel, and a tea trolley covered in brushes and twisted tubes of paint and stuff. The room was full of paintings, and every one of them was in the style of the Starving Artist picture we'd just given Downey. I sagged between Pete and Angie as I stared at the dozens and dozens of pictures covered in wiggly little maggoty shapes.

'You…collect them?' Angie said.

'My dad paints them.'

'These are your *dad's*?' I said as my stomach turned over.

'Yes.'

'You mean we gave you a picture your *dad* painted?' Pete said.

'Yes.'

'But I thought your dad was a farmer,' Angie said.

'This is what he does in his spare time.'

'Keeps me out of mischief,' said a new voice, behind us.

'I was just showing them your stuff, Dad,' Downey said.

'Fine. Introduce us, Neil.'

'Jiggy, Angie, Pete, my dad,' said Downey.

Mr Downey was the only member of the family who hadn't dressed for the occasion. He looked just as shabby and ragged as he did the last time we saw him, in the Starving Artists tent. He didn't recognise us, and we didn't mention that we'd just given the late birthday boy one of his paintings. Downey didn't either, which I was quite glad about.

'Not everyone's taste perhaps,' Mr Downey said, strolling round the room.

'No,' I said, trying not to look at them.

'They're very unusual,' Angie said. 'All those little abstract shapes.'

'Oh, they're not abstracts,' Mr Downey said. 'Multiple portraits, more like.'

'Portraits?'

'Would you like to meet my subjects?'

'Subjects?'

He left the room. We followed – slowly. This was getting weird.

'Just taking our visitors down the garden,' he said to his wife in the dining room.

'Oh, Ron,' she said, 'must you? This is Neil's party night.'

'I don't mind,' Neil piped up.

'You won't know we've gone,' Mr Downey said.

He stepped out the back door and marched up the path towards the big grey ugly building – a sort of concrete bunker – that we'd seen from the distance. 'You'll love this,' said Downey, running after his old man.

The sky had lightened again and the dark cloud had rolled away, taking the thunder with it. I glanced around at the empty black fields, wondering what sort of farmer Mr Downey was. No crops that I could see, and the only animals were up in the sky. All but one of the flying beasts were doing a sort of cha-cha along the distant horizon. The one that wasn't with them was a hippo, who'd flown back to take a turn at the sky-writing. It was zipping around up there like an old hand, white vapour streaming from its rear. So far it had written:

HE WHO STEALS FROM M

'Wonder what the M stands for?' Angie said.
'Me?' I said. '"He who steals from me"?'
'Could be. Yes, here comes an "e".'
'Sounds like the start of a threat.' I glanced at

Pete. 'Like "He who steals from me will be turned into a mountain goat with fleas".'

Pete gulped.

'Could explain the sudden thunder back then,' Angie said.

'What could?' I said.

'Well, if JR went back to the kennel and found the picture gone he probably blew a genie gasket, which made the thunder, and now he's looking for whoever swiped it. The picture.'

'You can't scare me,' said Pete, fooling no one.

Over at Number One, Sink Hole Drove, Mr Flowerdew had come out to his back garden to stare up at the sky. He probably didn't get to see too many sky-diving hippos that wrote notes with their back ends. Downey and his dad can't have seen the hippo at all, or the elephant, or the other flying animals, because they didn't look up once. All they seemed interested in was showing us the inside of their bunker. Mr D held the door open for us as we joined them. Metal door, rusty red colour. We entered. He punched a switch and two banks of strip lights flickered on, showing a gloomy interior containing twenty or so big tanks. As the door clanged shut behind us my nostrils flung themselves across my cheeks. So did Pete and Angie's. And we thought the *house* smelt bad?

'Come and see,' grinned Downey from the nearest tank. The smell didn't seem to affect him. Obviously used to it. Didn't notice it any more.

We joined him at the tank. It was stuffed with dead chickens, half eaten fish, sheep's heads, and various other bits and pieces that I didn't want to identify. It was horrible. Disgusting. And …jeepers-creepers the rotting flesh was…no, it couldn't be. But yes! It was moving. There were tiny creatures feeding on it. Squiggly-wiggly creatures, wriggling in and out of every wing, every dead bloodshot eye, every mouth, every…

Maggots.

Krillions and willions of maggots.

My last meal stirred in my stomach. My tongue filled my mouth. I squinted round at all the other tanks. Every one of them contained dead flesh crawling with maggots. There were more maggots under this roof than I could count in four lifetimes. I had come to the secret home of the vile creatures that haunted my sleeping mind. I stood at the rotting heart of...

Nightmare World.

Chapter Twenty-Two

When Mr Downey eventually got the message that watching maggots crawl in and out of dead meat isn't everyone's idea of a really fun thing to do, he opened the door and let us out. I glanced at Pete and Angie. The blood had drained from their faces, and their legs, like mine, seemed to want to go in any direction but forward. Mr Downey, maggot farmer, was talking excitedly. I would rather not have listened, but it seemed rude to cover my ears. Besides, my hands weren't working.

'I've been fascinated by maggots since I was a boy,' he said. 'Neil's the same, aren't you, son?'

'Yes, Dad.' I bet he hadn't told his father about slicing them in two on his Woodwork guillotine.

'To most people a maggot is a maggot, end of story,' Mr Downey said as we headed up the path to the house. 'But there are many different species, and each has its individual charms. *Cephalopina titillator*, for instance. Great favourite of mine. I keep a jar of them on my desk in the office. They're usually found in camels' nostrils, did you know that?'

'Nnnnnggghhh?' I said, fascinated.

'Nice and moist up there, I guess. And the rhinoceros botfly. Lovely little chap. Rich brown colour, grows up to five centimetres in length, squats in rhinos' stomachs.' He laughed gaily. 'A family of botflies once made its home in my left buttock. Don't ask me how they got there, but my wife, bless her, she squeezed the little tykes out, one by one.' He held the back door open for us. 'Now let's get stuck into that birthday tea! I'm for the sausages on sticks!'

I leant queasily against the wall to steady myself before following the others in. Up above, the hippo had finished its message and was lolloping away to join the others on the horizon. The complete message said:

HE WHO STEALS FROM ME SHALL BE PUNISHED

I didn't actually care just then. I went indoors wondering how I could face party food with my head full of maggots.

'Change of plan,' Mrs Downey said. 'The entertainer's all set up, didn't take long at all, so we're going to see the show first.'

I gasped with relief.

'You don't want to wait a bit and see if any other guests turn up?' Mr Downey asked her.

'I don't think it would be fair on Neil to wait any longer,' she said. 'No, let's get started.'

'Right oh. Come on, gang!'

Mr D headed for another room. His kids skipped after him. Pete, Angie and I didn't skip. Zombies whose sole ambition is to puke over the wallpaper don't do an awful lot of skipping.

The furniture in the front room had been pushed back to make room for the entertainment. Silky red and gold curtains had been drawn across the end of the room. They hung on portable rails that must have been carted in from the van outside, which could be seen through the window. There were pictures all over the van – a white rabbit in a top hat, fan-shaped decks of cards, coloured stars and comets, magic wands, stuff like that. And the words:

The Great Al Dente

Tinny music suddenly blared out from behind the curtains and Mrs Downey told us to sit down. There were only two chairs, and she and her husband grabbed them, so the rest of us had to flop down on the floor. What is it with adults? How is it they always get the chairs? At what point – tell me this, I'd really like to know – at what point does a kid qualify for a chair? Is there a special age or something? But it wasn't a chair I needed then, and it certainly wasn't a party magic show. It was a bed in a darkened room and total silence and a starvation diet for a month. But like the others I did as I was told and sat on the floor, and the curtains drew back, and there he was, the Great Al Dente, bowing low.

'Well, you said he did the occasional gig,' Angie whispered.

Yes, it was Mr Dent, all geniefied in fat pants, shoes with turned-up toes, turban covering the stopper hole in his forehead.

'His old uniform?' I said.

'Wouldn't mind betting,' said Ange.

'You two are so gullible,' said Pete.

To complete the genie look, Mr Dent wore a false

beard and moustache. He kept twirling the ends of the moustache and stroking the beard as he spoke in this deep foreign-sounding voice, and laughing this great booming laugh and strutting about with his hands on his hips like something out of a panto. He didn't let on that he knew any of us, treated us like total strangers as he ran through the usual card tricks, sawed a live rabbit in half and put it together again, tugged endless knotted scarves out of his sleeves. He did quite a bit more, but I still had maggots on my mind so I didn't concentrate much. Every now and then I shuddered at the memory of the bunker. Pete and Angie were already over it. Specially Pete. He wouldn't be Pete if he let something like that slow him down. Another Petey thing was the way he was watching the show. All superior, like this stuff was beneath him, too young for him.

But to finish his act, the Great Al Dente did something that even took my mind off the maggoty bunker. He unscrewed one of his hands and lobbed it at the audience. Suddenly we were holding a hand, a very real hand, moving fingers and all, that wasn't connected to a body. 'Argh! Eurgh!

Yurrukkkk!' we went, chucking it to one another because nobody could bear to touch it. From hand to hand went the hand, wriggling all the time, while we yelled and screamed with horror. Even Pete wasn't keen to hang on to it. 'It's probably 'armless!' he bawled, but still tossed it to the next person. Then, as suddenly as it had landed among us, the hand jumped away and scurried off on its fingertips, leapt up into the Great Al Dente's sleeve. He gave it a twist and held it up for us to marvel at, on the end of his arm.

I nudged Pete. 'Still think he's an ordinary mortal?'

'Huh!' He wouldn't admit it, even now.

The Great Al Dente gave a long showy bow and thanked us for coming in his deep phony accent. Mrs Downey led the applause, the silky red and gold curtains drew themselves across, and we filed out like good little kiddies to our even later late birthday tea.

There were the usual paper plates and party serviettes covered with little bears and candles for five-year-olds, and there was a big trifle, bowls of crisps, the sausages on sticks, and so on. We sat where Mrs D told us, Pete and Angie and me on one side of the table (me in the middle), the three Downey kids facing us like we were going to fight a duel with cheese straws. Mr Downey sat at one end, and when Mrs Downey parked herself at the other Pete took it for a signal to start, and grabbed a bundle of neat little triangular sandwiches and stuffed them in his mouth.

'For what we are about to receive,' Mrs Downey said suddenly.

Pete's bulging cheeks turned to stone. So did the hands of two other Brook Farm Estaters reaching for party fodder. We looked round the table. All Downey eyes were closed, all Downey fingers locked in pre-tea prayer. Angie and I drew our hands back and pulled faces at one another while Pete finished his mouthful in double-quick time.

When the thanks-a-bunch prayer was done, the Downey fingers unlocked and the Downey eyes opened and all the Downey teeth flashed. Pete and Angie and I were about to take a second stab at actually eating the late birthday tea when the lady of the house started singing and conducting 'Happy Birthday'. We joined in on the last line, quite a bit less than half-heartedly. As we came to the end something rumbled. I thought for a second it was Pete's stomach. But it wasn't Pete's stomach. It was thunder.

'Tuck in, tuck in!' cried Mrs D.

We tucked in, before she could dream up some other way to make us squirm. We'd demolished about half the stuff that was obviously intended for a dozen kids when the window darkened. I looked at it. The sky had clouded over, really clouded, cutting out almost all the daylight.

'Very changeable today,' said Mrs Downey.

She got up and turned the light on, then slipped out of the room. More thunder. I looked at the window again – just in time to be blinded by an angry flash of lightning. You know how you look at a brilliant light sometimes, and when you close your eyes you still see it, but in the opposite colour? Well, when I looked away from the window the lightning was still in my eyes, but instead of it just being a negative flash, it was now a word.

Gotcha!

I looked at Angie. She'd seen nothing. I looked at Pete. Nor had he.

'Birthday piii-eee!' said a sing-song voice: Mrs Downey, returning from the kitchen with a big dish, which she set down on the table.

'Ooooo,' said all the other Downeys, slapping their lips.

Mr D winked at us. 'Take my word for it, Edina's fruit pies are like nothing you ever tasted.'

It certainly looked good. Thick golden melt-in-the-mouth pastry, and when Mrs Downey sliced it down the middle, fruit of all kinds tumbled out like fat fruity bees from an exploding hive. So mouth-watering was this pie that the worrying word in the back of my eyes just popped out of existence. Mrs Downey divided half the pie into eight pieces. It was so big – made for all the guests that didn't turn up – that even an eighth part of half was a whacking portion. She dropped the eight slices into eight dishes and handed them round.

'Help yourselves to cream,' Mr Downey said, pointing to a jug.

We eagerly poured cream on our super-fruity

chunks of pie, and plunged our spoons in before Mrs D decided to say some more prayers. I glanced at the window as I raised mine to my mouth. The thunder and lightning had stopped. Everything was going to be OK after all. More than OK. I was about to stuff myself with the fruitiest pie ever made by human hand. I popped my spoon in my mouth, and—

'Where is my picture?'

My teeth clamped down on my spoon. Where had that little voice come from? I noticed a thin column of purple smoke dribbling out of the cream jug. In the smoke was a tiny JR, scowling up at me. He spoke again, in the same small voice.

'I *said*, where's my *picture?*'

The wonderful fruit pie slithered down untasted. I removed my spoon. Glanced round the table. No one had noticed the smoke. No one had seen him or heard him speak. But they would hear me – wouldn't they?

'How would I know where your picture is?'

'Oh you *know*,' he replied smokily.

Everyone else was still scoffing Mrs Downey's fruit pie and chatting like JR and I weren't there.

Even Pete and Angie. He must have put a spell on them so they wouldn't be aware of us. I turned back to him. He was small right now because it amused him to be small, but he was as powerful as ever, and in a dangerous mood. He'd worked out that one of us had taken his adopted painting. What he didn't know was what we'd done with it. The sensible thing would be to tell him, of course. Then he could go off with his picture and I could get back to the terrific fruit pie. But all of a sudden something came over me.

Anger.

I was so sick of being picked on all the time. I was even being picked on this time for something *Pete* had done. Enough was enough.

'You know, genie, you're starting to get on my nerves.'

Yes, that's what I said. And for about ten seconds nothing happened, nothing at all. Then the smoke drifting from the cream jug flared brightly, and when the flare died, the room darkened about me, like on a stage where everything goes black except the people in the spotlight. The others were outside the spotlight. Their voices faded. Total silence and darkness except for where JR and I

245

were. He was no longer small and swaddled in smoke. He leant against the wall in his teenage rig: torn jeans, chains, tattoos, face jewellery. The new him hadn't lasted long.

'Care to repeat that, man?' he said, chewing gum.

I had another chance. I could tell him where his picture was and get out of there without being turned into a wire coat hanger or something. And what did I say?

'I said you're starting to get on my nerves. But I was being kind. You're not just starting. You've been on them since you climbed out of that piddling Pool. Don't you get it? You're not wanted here. You're not liked. Go away. Find another soggy hole to live in. Leave me *alone*!'

Well, you know how it is. You lose your rag and say things you didn't even know were in your head, and then it's too late and your whole life has become cheese. But what do you think JR did when I shared all this with him? Did he become a huge terrifying ogre? Did he screw me into the wall with his thumb? Did he scatter my atoms and sweep them under the carpet with a dustpan and brush?

No. He relaxed. He smiled. He became the

friendliest I'd seen him.

'Seeing as I'm such a huggy-wuggy dude deep down,' he said, 'I'll pretend I didn't hear that, and make your dreams come true.'

'What?'

After all I'd said he was going to make my dreams come true?

'One of them anyway,' he added toothily.

'One of them?' Oh well, one dream come true was better than none. 'Um…any particular one?'

'Well, not a dream as *such*,' he said. 'I was thinking more of a…' He chewed slowly for a little while; then his friendly smile thinned out. 'More of a *nightmare*.'

Suddenly there was an ice cube where my heart used to be.

'You're going to make one of my *nightmares* come true?'

'That's right. Unless you'd care to tell me where my picture is…?'

And naturally I caved in and told him. Didn't I? Well, no actually. I blew my top again.

'I'm not telling you anything…man!'

'Oh. Shame.'

He fixed his eyes on me. Really fixed them. And what eyes. They'd never been so purple, and they were locked so tightly on mine that I couldn't blink or turn away. I felt his purple stare drill into my skull, tunnel right into my brain, creep around in there like a burglar in the dark, opening little doors and drawers, slamming them shut, moving on to another brainy junk room. I couldn't move or speak, but I could think, and one of the things I thought was: *If he can see what's in my head, why doesn't he look for info about the whereabouts of his painting?* All I could come up with was that he was too far out of his clogs to think of it.

'Got one,' he said at last.

I felt him pull out of my head. I blinked. I could move again. The room lightened. The dining table came back, and everyone around it. They were all still eating the wonderful fruit pie. I felt my hand twitch. It still held the spoon, and was heading for the pie in my dish. Except that the pie in my dish wasn't just fruit pie any more. It had an added ingredient.

Maggots.

'Pete,' I whispered hoarsely. 'Angie.'

They carried on eating like I'd ceased to exist. Their pie didn't have the extra ingredient. Nor did anyone else's. I gripped my spoon in a fist of iron. Tried to hold it back. I failed. The spoon reached the dish. It dipped, scooped, lifted. There was a little bit of pastry on the spoon, a bit of fruit, but mostly it was maggots, writhing, wriggling, tangled, and coming towards me.

'Oh no,' I said. 'No, not that. Noooo!'

I clamped my lips. The spoon reached them. Tapped against them as if asking to be let in. A couple of maggs climbed off and slithered on to my upper lip. My mouth trembled. It started to open.

'Last chance,' said JR.

Big of you, I thought. But did I give in? What do you think? This was a battle. He was my enemy. I shook my head.

'So be it.'

He pointed at my mouth. It opened. The maggots on my top lip curled round and slipped inside. The spoon followed them in, rested on my tongue for a sec, and slid out empty. My lips closed. I felt them moving in there. Wiggle-wiggle, wiggle-wiggle. And then...

I started munching.

Soft little innards squirted this way and that. Imagine squeezing his fat spots with your teeth and you've got it. And my taste buds snapped back into action. I'd missed out on the taste sensation of super-fruity fruit pie, but I got the full flavour of uncooked maggot. It was like... Let me see. You know what fresh roast chicken tastes like? Well it was nothing like that. It was like chewing underpants that had been worn day and night for a year.

The pie in my dish was almost entirely maggots now. My spoon dipped, scooped, headed back to me. My mouth opened to receive it. I couldn't keep it closed. In went the spoon, full. Out it came, empty. My lips slammed shut like prison gates. Maggots tussled on my tongue in the dark. Scaled the inner walls of my cheeks. Picked their way in and out of my teeth. Slithered around my quivering tonsils.

I got busy. Chomp, chomp, chomp.

I swallowed. Oozy, half chewed maggots went down, wriggling all the way.

But this didn't free up space in my mouth. Far

from it. The more I ate the more there seemed to be in there. I crunched again.

Skwelsh!

And again.

Skwoosh!

Munch, munch, munch.

Down, down, down. Dozens and dozens and dozens. Squirming.

My stomach was doing multiple somersaults. I wanted to chuck up. I wanted to spew. I wanted to heave and hurl till I could heave and hurl no more.

But I couldn't. All I could do was eat. Eat maggot pie.

For real.

Chapter Twenty-Three

He'd won. No question. I didn't stand a chance against a genie as mean and powerful as him.

'All right, I'll show you where your rotten picture is!'

This may not have sounded the way it reads, because it's kind of hard to speak clearly when your mouth's crammed with maggots. Try it sometime. I kicked my chair back and jumped to my feet. Still no one noticed or heard me. I ran to the door.

'Don't forget your pie!' JR called after me.

I cursed him, but ran back to the table. Had to, no choice, couldn't leave till I'd had some more maggot pie. This time I didn't use the spoon. I plunged my hands in, grabbed as much as I could, jammed it into my mouth. Munching maggots like a maniac, I spun out of the room and ran down the hall. I wanted this over with. I shot into the room where Mr Downey painted his pictures. JR arrived seconds later.

'Take your pick, piddle-brain!' I cried maggotly.

When he saw all the paintings just like his, his dreadlocks lit up at the ends like a fibre optics lamp. He came in. Strolled round, gaping. I let him get on with it, chewing quietly. Something moved in the doorway. It was the Great Al Dente, still in the phony face fungus and genie gear. Of course! Mr Dent, the one person on the planet who could put a genie in the dole queue! He gasped when he saw the maggots wriggling in my teeth – the tea-table spell obviously hadn't included him. While he was still gawping, I ran to him, grabbed his wrist, lugged it across the room. JR turned as we approached. Stared at the unexpected genie type coming towards him. Before he could make a break for it I jerked the Dent hand that last stretch hoping it wouldn't come off again (it didn't) and slapped it on JR's shoulder.

'Die, fiend! Die! Die!' (I'd always wanted to say that).

'Why is this man's hand on my shoulder?' JR asked.

'Take a flying guess, ho-ho-ho,' I gloated through my maggots.

The Great Al Dente stood with his hand on JR's

shoulder. JR stood looking at it. I just stood, waiting. Was the Genie Touch working? Was he turning into an unsupernatural being? How could you tell? He already looked human in a teenage sort of way.

It was JR himself who broke the silence.

'Ah! I see! You thought that this fraud in fancy dress would just have to touch me and I'd lose my powers!'

I swallowed a throatful of my little chums and picked a couple out of my nose.

'That's right! And how does it *feel*, Mr Nobody Special?'

He removed the Great Al Dente's mitt from his shoulder. Then he picked up one of Mr Downey's paintings and took it to the window to examine it.

'How does it feel? No different at all. Now I wonder why that is?'

Behind him the sun was setting over the maggot bunker, dazzling me a bit. A frown lugged my eyes together. I'd just caught up with what he said half a minute earlier. '*This fraud in fancy dress.*' Fraud? Hadn't he recognised Mr Dent in the genie togs? I glanced at the Great Al Dente. He wasn't doing much, just standing with his hands at his sides, staring at the maggots in my teeth. But suddenly his attention flipped from me to JR, who'd put the painting down and was waggling his fingers. When they stopped waggling JR was dressed like Mr Dent. Exactly like. He even had a false beard and moustache. The Great Al Dente's eyes went so wide that he didn't notice when one of his contact lenses popped out. For the first time I got a glimpse of one of his uncontacted eyes. It was blue. Not as blue as the dropped contact, but still blue enough not to be called purple. Which meant...

Mr Dent gave a little whimper. I almost whimpered myself when I saw why. JR's head was turning round. All the way round, slowly, on his neck. He was showing me that he was still in business. His head started to turn faster, then faster still, until it was whizzing round at such speed you could have mistaken it for a spinning top in a turban. The Great Al Dente spoke – 'Yawp!' – and dived out of the room, taking my last hope with him. Pete had been right. He wasn't an ex-genie. Never had been a genie. He was a retired stage magician with a bunch of tricks, that's all. The dent in his head was just a dent in his head. Maybe he'd been dropped on a hard-boiled egg as a baby, when his skull was soft, who knows? How could I have got it so wrong? JR had told me that Mr Dent had the lethal Genie Touch and I'd believed him. There was probably no such thing. He'd been stringing me along. Why? For a laugh? Because it gave him a kick? Questions, questions, and no answers, answers.

JR's head slowed down. It stopped, facing out the window. He jerked it round with his hands. The purple eyes found mine.

'What am I going to do with you, O Master?'

'Haven't you done enough?' I spluttered tragically.

'Obviously not.'

Something moved outside, in the bright low sunlight. Or maybe it didn't. Easy to imagine things when the sun's in your eyes. I didn't imagine JR waving his fingers at all the paintings though, or the tiny shapes in them turning into real live multicoloured maggots which fell out of the frames and headed in my direction.

'Jig?'

I glanced at the door. Pete and Angie. The spell JR had put on them had worn off.

'Help,' I said.

They didn't help. They pointed at my feet. I looked down. The first wave of maggots was crawling over my trainers. I tried to kick them off but my feet wouldn't move. They reached my ankles, wiggled up into the legs of my jeans. Normally in a situation like this I would be hopping around like a hot-wired kangaroo by now, but I was rooted to the spot as surely as if my feet had been stapled to the floorboards. I had no choice but to stand absolutely still while more and more maggots crawled out of the paintings, across the floor, up me. In minutes every centimetre of me would be covered. And then...

I would become maggot pie myself.

I heard a chuckle over by the window. JR stood with his arms folded over his chest like a pantomime genie. He was enjoying this.

But then several things happened, one after the other. Very unexpected things. The first was a cry of 'One for all and all for lunch!' as Angie snatched up the room's only chair and rushed forward, smashing it down on the endless stream of McCue-hungry maggots. The second thing was that JR stopped laughing and grabbed the window-ledge as if his legs had been whipped from under him. His false beard fell off. Then someone outside, someone with the sun behind him, leaned in the window just long enough to tweak my ex-genie's ear before going back out of sight. JR clutched the tweaked ear in horror. As he did this, the maggots on their way to me stopped in their tracks. They turned round, started back the way they'd come. The ones that had already reached me dropped off and joined them. Back they all streamed towards the picture frames. When they reached them they climbed back in, found their old places, and turned to paint again. There were a few gaps. These were where the squashed ones on the floor had been. Something popped in my mouth. A number of somethings. The maggots still in there were exploding like little pellets of fizzy sherbet. It was over.

'Did you see the tweaker at the window?' Angie said in amazement.

Oh, I'd seen all right. So had Pete.

'The sun was in my eyes,' he said, 'but I could swear it was…'

'It was,' whispered Ange.

I was as flabbergasted as they were, but I didn't want to speak just then. I'd never realised how good it was to have a mouth free of maggots. My saliva still tasted like used underwear, but at least I didn't have to share it with other life forms.

We turned to look at JR. He was feebly waving his hands about and chanting spells or whatever in that old genie lingo of his. They didn't work. Nothing worked. Even his dreadlocks drooped lifelessly.

'Anyone seen a blue contact lens?'

Mr Dent. He was still in costume, though the beard and moustache were a little skewed. He looked weird with eyes of different shades of blue. I pointed at the bright blue contact on the floor. He picked it up, wiped it with a moistened finger, slotted it back in place.

'Seems I'm not the only entertainer here today.'

'You mean the head-spinning quick-change artist?' I said.

He nodded. 'Had me really spooked for a minute. But you too. The maggots in the mouth trick. How did you *do* that? You quite put me to shame, you two.'

'We were just fooling around. Your act was great.

Specially the hand stunt.'

'Yes,' said Angie. 'Loved the hand stunt.'

Mr Dent smiled – 'Thanks' – but you could tell he felt outclassed. 'Think I'll go to the pub and drown my sorrows.'

'Dressed like that?' said Pete.

'Past caring.'

He went. I turned to see what JR was doing now. He wasn't there.

'What happened to him?'

'Climbed out the window,' Angie said.

I went to the window. JR was stumbling across the empty black fields. As I watched he hurled his turban away in fury. Every now and then he flung his hands in the air and shouted something Mongolian. Nothing happened, nothing changed. He was stuck in the unmagical body of a seventeen-year-old boy. From now on he would have to live the life of a real human being. I felt almost sorry for him.

260

Chapter Twenty-Four

The spell that JR had put on the others in the dining room had worn off with Pete and Angie first, I don't know why, maybe because they'd been under one of his spells before. When they snapped out of it and found me missing and the Downeys carrying on as if I was still there, they knew something had happened and came looking for me. By the time the three of us returned to the dining room, the Downeys had come out of the spell too and started to wonder why there were suddenly only five of them.

'Didn't see you go,' said Neil. 'One minute you're here, the next you're not. How'd you do that?'

'Ask the Great Al Dente,' I said. 'What a *magician!*'

He looked pleased. 'You know who he is, don't you?' he said as we sat down again.

'No, Neil, who is he?' (Angie, all innocent.)

'Mr Dent!' said Downey.

'Mr Dent?' (Me, all round-eyed.)

'Yes. Really. It's Mr Dent from school!'

'Wow, never've guessed.' (Pete, all unimpressed.)

'You haven't finished your pie, Jiggy,' Mrs Downey said. 'Don't you like it?'

Mine was the only bowl that still had some pie in it. It was pure fruit again, not a maggot in sight, but I'd kind of gone off it. I didn't tell her this, of course. Told her it was the most absolutely incredible fruit pie ever, but I have a delicate stomach which can't handle too much absolute incredibleness, which left her with a pleased smile on her face.

After that it was Embarrassing Party Games. Pete flatly refused to take part in any of them, but Angie and I did our best to look like we enjoyed behaving like complete and utter wallies. 'Is there no *end* to this?' she growled as we passed a balloon from chest to chest in a jolly circle of us and the Downey kids.

But it ended eventually, and we headed for the door, thanking everyone for a really terrific time, trying not to skip for joy.

'I'll give you a lift home,' Mr Downey said.

'S'all right, thanks a lot, but the air will do us good.'

'I insist.'

He had a white van with the words DOWNEY'S MAGGOTS on the side, which I wish I'd seen earlier, then I could have run a mile. There was just room on the long front seat for the three of us and the driver. The smell in there was pure bunker. It was hard to keep the retching noises down. Mrs Downey and the junior Downeys came to the gate to wave us off with happy smiles.

The van bumped us back along Sink Hole Drove, past Mr Flowerdew's house – we looked for him, no sign – and across the wasteland where the brick works used to be. Over to one side, near the new leisure centre, we saw JR standing by what was left of the Piddle Pool. He'd got shot of most of the genie togs by now. Looked sort of lost standing there in boxer shorts and a T-shirt.

'Hope he's not planning a dip in there,' Mr Downey said with a laugh.

The idea worked for Pete. He leaned out of the window. 'Take a dive, riddle-head! Take a big long drink! Hope it chokes you!'

Mr Downey's laugh became a cough and he put his foot down in case JR turned out to be a violent psycho who might run after the van and scratch it with a coin.

When we reached the estate we asked to be dropped off at the first houses. We needed a few minutes to ourselves before facing our parents. So much had happened in the past couple of hours that we'd almost forgotten why we'd been so keen to go to the party, but it came flooding back once we were on home ground.

'Mother Hubbard will have been and gone,' I said. 'He'll have told our parents everything. They'll be waiting for us with hatchets.'

'Let's go and sit in the park for a day or two till they get over it,' Pete suggested.

'No,' Angie said firmly. 'We have to face this.'

'Can't you face it for all of us?' I said.

'Oh, boys are such *wimps*!' she said. 'What we do is, we get the Golden Oldie rollicking out of the way, then meet up, or phone, and go over the latest bombshell. We can't go to school ever again unless we get our heads round this.'

'In that case I don't want to get my head round it,' said Pete.

When we reached our street we found something

unusual in the road outside my house. A heap o
twisted metal that had once been a car.

'Looks like your dad's done another trade-in,'
Angie said.

They went to their house and I walked with
leaden feet up the path of *The Dorks*. I had a front-
door key for a change. I planned to use it and sneak
up very quietly to my room without being heard. I
opened the door. Silently. And found Mum and
Dad standing shoulder to shoulder in the hall,
waiting for me. They didn't look happy. But they
didn't look angry either, which I thought was quite
odd. Looked more like the bearers of bad news,
such as the date of my execution.

'Have you heard?' Mum said.

'Not yet,' I said.

'About Mr Hubbard,' said Dad.

I got ready to run past them up the stairs and
lock myself in the bathroom for ever.

'OK, get it over with.'

'He's been hit by a roof-rack,' Mum said.

'Er?'

'Don't know what he was doing here,' Dad said,
'but he'd parked his car out there in the street and

...en this bolt of lightning struck it.'

...et?'

...car. Completely demolished it.'

'The roof-rack came off and cracked him on the head,' Mum explained.

My face must have lit up, because they looked quite shocked when I said: 'Is he dead?'

'No, he's not dead,' Mum said. 'But he's in hospital, concussed. Could be there for days, apparently.'

'Great!'

I bounded into the kitchen for a swig of junior bubbly. Now I had two things to celebrate. I no longer had a mean genie on my case, and I still had my reputation as a perfect student, at home anyway. My luck seemed to be on the up. Wow. New experience, and by jiminy I liked it. Bottle in hand, I wandered out to the back garden and stood before the kennel. Now that JR was stuck in a human body he'd be too big to get through its door, and he sure couldn't materialise inside without magic, so it stood to reason that he'd find somewhere else to doss. That meant that Stallone could live there after all. I wouldn't charge him

266

much. For all I knew he'd heard the news and moved in already.

I got down on one knee to peek in the kennel. Nothing had changed since I last looked, except that the maggot painting wasn't on the wall and there was a new rug on the floor. The rug was like one of those stretched-out tiger skins you see in films about hunters, only it wasn't as big as a tiger skin, or the same colour. It had four outstretched legs and a tail though. And a head. The head was the only part that wasn't as flat as a pancake. It was propped up on its chin so that the glassy eyes stared at you. Stared at me. Couldn't see me though. Stallone's eyes were as dead as his flattened body.

Pete and Angie came over soon after. They were as delirious as I was that Mother Hubbard hadn't made it through our front doors, though Angie wondered if we should send him a Get Well card. Pete wasn't keen.

'He's our headteacher. He was going to shop us to our parents. Do they make Stay Sick cards?'

I took them out back and showed them the new

Stallone. Angie was devastated – she was one of the few people that got on with him – but Pete cheered. I'd never been that close to Stallone myself, but nobody should end their days as a rug.

'You were probably the last person to see him alive,' I said to Pete.

'Hey, don't blame me for this,' he said.

'I mean when you came back for the Starving Artist painting. You said he was here then. My bet is, JR came home shortly after you nicked the painting, found him in his kennel, and rugged him. He said he would if he ever saw the mad mog here again.'

'What are you going to do with him?' Angie asked.

I shrugged. 'What *can* you do with a flattened cat?'

'He'd make a wicked toilet-seat cover,' said Pete.

There was a little knocking sound in the distance. We trooped round to the gate and unbolted it. We had a visitor. A visitor in shorts and a fancy shirt.

'Hello, sir,' I said. 'Didn't expect to see you here.'

'I thought I ought to pay you a visit as soon as possible,' he said. 'Can we have a chat?'

'What, here?'

'I was thinking somewhere less public.'

'We just got in,' Angie said. 'Our folks won't let us out again this late.'

'They won't even know you've gone.'

He took his dark glasses off and put them in his shirt pocket. Having seen him at the Downeys' window giving JR's ear the Genie Touch that drained him of his powers, the purple eyes came as no surprise, but it was still a pretty shocking sight. We got over it soon enough, though, because Mr Flowerdew waved a hand, muttered something foreign, and next thing we knew...

Chapter Twenty-Five

…we were on a tropical island. The kind you see in travel brochures but never expect to see in real life. We stood, the four of us, on a long white beach with palm trees, gulls swooping around a huge gorgeous sun as it sank into the brilliant blue ocean. Pete gave a whoop and started running up and down and rolling over and over in the sand. Angie and I just gaped happily.

'Good choice,' I said to Mr Flowerdew.

'An indulgence,' he answered. 'I've been without any real power for so long that…' He looked about him with the biggest smile I'd ever seen on his face. 'You're not taken aback by any of this, are you? I'm not wrong about you three? You do know about genies?'

'Only the stuff we picked up from JR,' Angie said.

'JR? That's what he calls himself? And you knew what he was?'

'Oh yes. Jig was his master.'

'I knew one of you was. I sensed the connection when I touched him.'

'How did you know to come to the Downeys' house and give him the Touch?' I asked.

'I've been coming over faint at odd moments these past couple of days,' Mr Flowerdew said. 'It felt as if some force was affecting me, but it didn't occur to me that it was a genie until you let it slip that there was one about and drew my attention to the flying animals. Once I knew my incapacity was caused by the proximity of a practising genie I was able to track him by the power he radiated.'

'To the house next door,' Angie said.

'To the house next door.'

'But why did you put him out of business?' I asked. 'I mean how did you know it was the right thing to do?'

'I've been human long enough to know that one thing the world doesn't need is a powerful genie that likes playing pranks.'

A couple of other things made sense now too. All along we'd thought that JR thought Mr Dent was a genie. What dummies. Mr Dent was never weakened when JR was near, but Mr Flowerdew was. When JR appeared at the old Woodwork shop without his usual powers it wasn't Mr Dent he was hiding from, but Flowerdew, who he must have seen or sensed nearby. And it was because JR was near that Mr F was so wobbly on his pins when he looked in – and when he tottered out of the Science lab too.

'You,' I said. 'A genie. You of all people.'

'Well I'm not one now,' he said. 'Haven't been for years, ever since I myself received the Genie Touch.'

'Another genie touched you and zapped *your* powers?' Angie said.

'Oh, not deliberately, but the end result was the same. He bumped into me one evening, coming round a corner. He was in the form of a pizza-delivery girl. By the time his pizzas hit the pavement I was virtually powerless. He was very apologetic.'

'But you didn't lose all your powers?' I said, remembering what JR had said about this. 'Not quite?'

'No, not quite. Even decommissioned genies retain some small no-account ability. Mine turned out to be green fingers.'

272

'You have green fingers?' Pete cried, bounding back along the beach. 'Show me, show me!'

'He means he's a natural with flowers and stuff,' said Angie.

'Oh, that,' he said, disappointed.

'I wasn't too pleased at first,' Mr Flowerdew said. 'The form I was wearing at the time – this one – wasn't the healthiest specimen. But over the years I've come to rather enjoy being human, even within the limitations of this weak and feeble body.'

'You look better now,' I said. 'I've never seen you so healthy-looking.'

'That's because some of your genie's strength and power has passed to me. Not a lot, but enough to make me feel better than I ever have in this form. The good health should remain, but the power will quickly fade – which is why I needed to see you urgently. I must use some of it to wipe your memories.'

'Do what?' said Pete.

'I have to if I'm to continue the life I've become accustomed to. I can't have you three coming into my class knowing I'm not who I pretend to be.'

'We won't tell anyone,' Angie said.

He shook his head. 'Sorry.' He looked it too. I mean genuinely. 'But I'd like to offer you something by way of compensation. I imagine you've not had an easy time at the hands of…what was his name again?'

'JR,' I said. 'No, not an easy time.'

'What sort of compensation?' Pete asked, suddenly interested.

'Three wishes,' Mr Flowerdew said.

'Three wishes?' I said. 'Each?'

'In total. One of you can have all of them, or you can have one each, it's up to you.'

'I vote I get all three,' said Pete.

'In your dreams,' said Angie.

'One each please,' I said to Mr Flowerdew.

'Your wishes are my command,' he replied with a smile.

'Can we wish for anything we like?' Pete wanted to know.

'Yes, but try and be reasonable. These temporary powers aren't as vast as full power. Some things might be beyond me.'

'How about luck?' I said. 'Could you make a person lucky if he wished for it?'

'I think I could manage that.' My heart thumped. 'But I should warn you all, now that you've accepted my offer you must be very careful what you say. Careless use of the word "wish" could lead to disappointment.'

'You don't have to tell *me*,' I said.

'Yeah, but that's you,' sneered Pete. 'You won't catch *me* flushing my one and only you-know-what down the pan.'

'Can I ask a question before making my wish?' Angie asked.

'Certainly,' said Mr F. 'Just don't use the word "wish" when you ask it.'

'Will everything JR did be wiped out now that he's no longer a genie?'

'Things he instigated or changed for his own amusement or benefit should return to their former state. The flying animals, for instance. The last I saw of them they were floating to earth and the Zoo people were rounding them up.'

'Does that mean,' Angie said, 'that if he made *us* do something it might not go back to the way it was before?'

'Genieology is an imprecise science,' Mr

Flowerdew said, 'but it seems likely that anything you did will stay as you left it.'

'So if we'd said something to upset someone, or if we'd flooded the school, people would remember who'd said it, who turned the taps on?'

'I'm afraid so, yes. Oh, so the flooding was the genie's doing too!'

'What about my cat?' I asked.

'Your cat?' said Mr Flowerdew.

'JR killed him.'

'Ah. Sorry to hear that. But unnatural death can only be undone by another wish, I'm afraid. Talking of which...who's first?'

'I've got mine ready,' Angie said.

'Go ahead then.'

'I wish that no one could remember the things JR made us do or say.'

It was such a small wish. She could have wished for anything – a really rosy future for herself, bundles of money, great happiness, stuff like that – but all she'd wished for was that our teachers wouldn't think badly of us for what had happened at school. I tell you, it brought tears to my eyes, that wish.

Mr Flowerdew waved his fingers, muttered

some genie words, and said: 'It's done.'

I smiled to myself. Now even Mother Hubbard, when he came to, would have forgotten why he wanted to see our parents.

'Who's next?' said Mr Flowerdew.

'Me, me,' said Pete, shoving me aside.

'Hold on to your wigs,' I said. 'The world's about to change. Pete Garrett's going to ask not to have to wash up every Tuesday.'

Pete came over all cocky. 'You think I'll waste it, don't you? Think I'll throw my wish away, like you did. Well think again, McCue. *You're* the kind of berk who says stupid things like "I wish I had six pairs of blue socks", not me.'

Mr Flowerdew muttered, waved his fingers, and said: 'Next.'

'Ready,' said Pete. 'God, my feet are hot. I wish I could—'

'You've had yours,' Mr F said, looking down.

Pete also looked down. So did Ange and I, at Pete's suddenly bulgy feet. He was wearing six pairs of blue socks, one on top of the other.

'No, no,' he said. 'That wasn't my wish, I was just saying—'

277

'What you said,' Angie reminded him, 'was: "I wish I had six pairs of blue socks." Congratulations. Your wish came true.'

'That's not fair!' Pete shouted.

'Seems fair to me,' I said.

He trudged through the sand to the nearest palm tree and started banging his head slowly against it.

'Last wish,' Mr Flowerdew said, turning to me.

I took a deep breath. Then I took another. I was being given a second chance. My life was going to go the way I wanted after all. I was going to get all the good luck I thought I'd missed out on by not peeing in the Piddle Pool the night before I started Infant School. One little wish and I would be the luckiest kid in town. The world.

'I wish...'

I paused. This was a big moment. I wanted to taste every word as I said it. I wanted to *feel* my luck change.

'What are you waiting for?' Pete snapped from his palm tree. 'Spit it out, so we can get out of this dump.'

I looked about me. Some dump. The long white

278

beach, the leaning palms, the great big beautiful sky, the golden sun dissolving into the sparkling blue ocean. A lot of people never get to see sights like that outside of picture postcards or TV. That made me luckier than them. Then I thought about the Brook Farm Estate. We had a nice house and our very own garden gnome, and I had two parents who could have been worse. And school. I moan about it all the time, but hey, gives me something to do. When you look at it like that there's stacks of people worse off than me. Yeah. I'm not so unlucky.

'I wish...' I said slowly.

'Will you just *say* it!' Pete bawled.

'I wish my cat hadn't been turned into a rug.'

'You *what?*' Pete said, falling down in a heap of amazement.

Mr Flowerdew waved his fingers, and said: 'Done.'

'Oh, Jig!' Angie said, and chucked her arms round my neck.

I felt a blush coming on. I grabbed her by the wrists and tore her arms away. Musketeers don't hug, never ever, specially one another. I would have to put that in the rule book.

'Just one more thing to do,' Mr Flowerdew said. 'I must cleanse your memories of everything to do with genies that isn't in stories or on the stage.'

'Go ahead,' said Pete miserably. 'I don't want to remember *any* of this.'

'I'd better get you home first. I feel my powers waning. We don't want to be stuck here, do we?'

'Worse places,' Angie said, gazing soulfully about her.

'Is there time for a quick paddle?' I said.

'Best not. Five more minutes and I'll once again be good for nothing but horticulture and teaching Science.'

He flapped his hands, mumbled, and we were once again at my back gate. He looked winded. He was sweating a bit.

'Took a lot out of me, that did. Silly of me to use so much power on a trip to the seaside.'

'Worth it, though,' I said.

He smiled. 'Yes, it was, wasn't it?'

'Do you still have enough power to wipe our memories, sir?' Angie asked.

'Hopefully. But I don't think I can manage you all at once. Have to attend to you one at a time.'

He did Pete first, then Angie. He didn't wave his hands and mutter this time, just put his fingertips on their temples and closed his eyes, lips moving silently.

'Are we supposed to feel different?' Pete said right away. 'I don't. I remember everything.'

'I'm so drained that I've had to use a slow-acting mind-wipe,' Mr Flowerdew said. 'Your memories should be genie-free by morning.' He turned to me. 'This one will just about finish me off.'

He put his fingertips on my temple, closed his eyes, moved his lips. I felt a slight vibration where he touched me, but that was all. He looked very weak when he'd finished.

'There we are,' he said then. 'When we meet again I'll be just another boring old teacher.'

'Any idea what'll become of JR?' I asked him.

'Who cares?' said Pete.

'He'll have to adjust to being human, as I did,' said Mr Flowerdew. 'It's not such a bad life. See you at school!'

He stepped back. I closed the gate on him. We strolled round the corner of the garden.

'Quite a day,' Angie said.

'Don't rub it in,' said Pete. 'I just can't believe I *did* that!' He sat down on the path and tore all his socks off.

As Angie and I approached the kennel a dark shape appeared in the doorway.

'Stallone!' I cried, running to him and falling to my knees and pulling his born-again head into my chest.

He must have felt pretty much like I did when Angie hugged me, but he didn't blush. He snarled and squirmed out of my arms, then ran straight between the legs that had appeared on the patio. Mum's legs. She almost went head first into her rockery.

'Uh-oh, just remembered something.' This was Pete. He'd stuffed his wish-socks in his pockets and was backing away towards the gate, looking up at the house.

'What?' I said.

'Me too,' said Angie, also looking up, also backing away.

'*What!*' I said.

But they were gone. Why were they in such a hurry? What had they remembered? I looked up at the house, at my window. Realised.

'Enjoy the party?' Mum asked as I ducked under her arm.

'Terrific. Event of the year. Real gourmet nosh.'

I charged up to my room. Stood stroking my chin for about twenty-five seconds before deciding what had to be done. I grabbed the stone as big as a fist and shoved it under my pillow, then ran to the top of the stairs.

'Mum! Dad! What have you done to my window?!'

Mum appeared down in the hall.

'Your window?'

'Yes! How did it get broken?'

'Broken?' said Dad, joining her from somewhere. 'Your window's broken?'

'Don't tell me you didn't know,' I said.

They started up, puzzled. Mum stopped halfway.

'Is this sand on the stairs?'

'Sand?' I said. 'What would sand be doing on the stairs?'

They reached the landing and came into my room. Stopped just inside the door, staring at the shattered window, which gave me a chance to go

283

on and on about leaving them in charge of the house for five minutes, just *five minutes*, and they let my window get broken. 'Parents these days,' I said. 'No sense of responsibility.' Just before they got their sad old wits back and ordered me to fill in an incriminating questionnaire, I came up with the forehead-slapping brainwave that the lightning must have done it. Well if lightning could pulp a car, I said to them, a window would be child's play. They agreed that it couldn't have been anything else, and by the time I went to bed Mum had cleared away all the broken glass and vacuumed the carpet, and Dad had nailed a piece of badly cut hardboard over the hole. I sighed when I saw it. My father isn't exactly a DIY wiz. That hardboard will probably still be there the day I pack my bags and leave home for good.

Chapter Twenty-Six

Next morning I inspected the kennel. The inside was normal again, proper size, and all the things JR put in it were gone. Shame really. There can't be many dog kennels that are furnished and decorated and bigger inside than out. Stallone didn't move in after all. Perhaps he didn't like it without the home comforts and space. Or maybe something told him that kennels are pretty cool places to avoid if you're a cat. As for JR, he seemed to disappear off the face of the earth after Mr Flowerdew pulled his plug. Or should that be lug?

You're probably wondering how I still knew about genies and all. Hadn't Mr Flowerdew wiped our memories? Well, he'd certainly wiped Pete and Angie's, but his juice must have been at a really low ebb when he got to me because I could still remember every detail, sharp as a needle in the behind. I tried a couple of test questions on Pete and Angie to see if I could jog anything, but they thought I was even nuttier than usual talking about genies with purple eyes and wishes and stuff, so I dropped the subject.

So now you know why I had to tell you all this. Because there's no one else to talk to about it. You have to agree, it's too much for one person to carry in his head alone. Drive him crazy. I didn't let on to Mr Flowerdew that he hadn't managed to wipe my mind. He stayed healthier-looking, and I was glad about that, but to this day he hasn't the faintest idea that I know what he used to be.

About a week after Mr F got rid of JR, there was a Teacher Training Day at school, which meant all the kids had a day off. Teacher Training Days happen quite often at Ranting Lane and they worry me a bit. I mean aren't teachers *already* trained? If not, what are they doing teaching us? Or maybe they're training to be something else, like, say, hairdressers. But you don't ask questions when you get a free day, just button it and keep well away from school in case they change their minds. Because we had this extra school-free time Pete and Angie and I thought we'd check out the swimming pool at the new leisure centre. It had only been open a day or two and this was the first chance we'd had to see it. When we arrived we saw that the car park was finished. Tarmac stretched right across where the Piddle Pool used to be. Sad really. I'd grown up with the Piddle Pool. There was nowhere away from home that I'd peed more.

The smell of chlorine, heated water and paint hit you when you went through the swimming-pool doors. We paid the entrance fee and Angie went to her changing room and Pete and I went to ours. We'd put our trunks on under our jeans to save time, so we were out first. We stood on the edge for a sec, looking the pool over. It was pretty smart. Big and bright and blue, with fake palm trees at all four corners. There were only three other people in the water – pesky adults – when we jumped in. There was a piercing whistle right away. We ignored it, and started splashing one another like crazy. Piercing whistle again, plus bellowing voice.

'NO JUMPING! NO SPLASHING!'

Pete carried on splashing, but I froze. I knew that voice. I dashed the water from my eyes, peered at the attendant on the high stool at the side of the pool. He was dressed in a red sports shirt, blue shorts, white deck shoes, wraparound sunglasses. It was JR, minus dreadlocks. He'd trimmed his hair right down and dyed it blond.

'I SAID NO *SPLASHING*!!!' he yelled at Pete as I swam to the side.

'Well, well,' I said, looking up at my ex-Humble Servant and Enemy.

JR tried to place my face through his shades. It must have looked pretty much the way it did the first time he saw it, water running down it, wet hair in my eyes. Then...

'You,' he said softly.

'And you. Working for a living. Here, of all places.'

'I have rent to pay now. A living to earn.'

Pete swam up behind me.

'Problem, Jig?'

He didn't know JR. Didn't know that he'd ever been anything but a swimming-pool attendant.

'No, just chatting.'

He wasn't having it. Pete doesn't like being told what to do. He curled his lip at JR.

'So what is it? Brand new pool, hardly anyone in it, and we're not allowed to rustle the *water*?'

'Regulations,' JR said.

'Yeah, right, regulations. Heard that before. I thought this was supposed to be a free country.'

'It's not a free pool.'

There was a mighty splash at the deep end.

'NO JUMPING IN!' JR yelled.

'What?!' Angie spluttered in the distance.

The adults in the pool climbed out. They didn't look very happy about sharing it with three innocent kids. Pete swam off to join Ange.

'Your belligerent friend doesn't seem to remember me,' JR said.

'You've been wiped from his memory.'

'But not yours?'

'Nothing can wipe you from my memory.'

'I'm touched.'

'We always thought so.'

He smiled and started down his little ladder from the high stool. It wasn't a friendly smile, but he didn't scare me now.

'How does it feel to be totally human?' I asked. 'No changing into anything you fancy now, eh?'

'No,' he said. 'What you see is what you get. It's not a very thrilling existence.'

He came to the edge of the pool and squatted there, bouncing on his calves, whistle dangling from his neck on a blue ribbon. There was a name badge pinned to his shirt. The name on it was James Riddle.

'So you're absolutely powerless?' I said.

'Apart from one tiny little ability, yes.'

'Oh yes, the Last Skill.'

I remembered Mr Flowerdew's way with flowers. Well, a power like that couldn't harm anyone. I deliberately splashed JR's deck shoes.

'What?' I said. 'You can reach the high notes in opera? Walk upside down on the high wire? Do a thousand and one press-ups without getting out of breath?'

He looked at his wet shoes. 'My ability is a little more personal than that. A small reminder of what I was, where I came from.'

'You came from a pool of piddle,' I said.

'So I did.'

I laughed. It was good to have the last laugh on someone who'd flattened my cat, made me cheek a

290

favourite teacher, removed my hair and replaced it with grass, someone who – worst of all – had made me eat maggot pie.

'Well whatever it is,' I said, 'it can't hurt me. So long, has-been!'

As I pushed away from the side I saw him lean over and whisk his hand in the water. Ripples spread outward. Normal enough, except... I looked harder. The tiles of the pool were blue, which made the water look blue, but the ripples JR made were a dirty yellow colour, and they were coming my way. I kicked my legs, but I'm not a great swimmer. The yellow ripples overtook me, encircled me and held me there like watery chains. I heard a yell, two yells –

'This pool is disgusting!'

'Jig, get out of there!'

– as Pete and Angie hauled them selves out at speed.

I tried to answer, but there was water in my mouth. Dirty yellow water. So this was JR's last small power: the ability to turn water into pee. And I was up to my neck in it. Up to my neck in a wide-awake nightmare at least as bad as being forced to scoff maggot pie. What was that I said about the last laugh? I should have known better. Last laughs don't happen to kids like me. Kids unlucky enough to be called...

Jiggy McCue

Turn the page
to find out about
Jiggy McCue's other
outrageously funny
and wildly wacky
adventures...

1 86039 836 7   £4.99

Something's after Jiggy McCue!
Something big and angry and invisible.
Something which hisses and flaps and stabs
his bum and generally tries to make
his life a misery. Where did it come from?

Jiggy calls in The Three Musketeers – One for
all and all for lunch! – and they set out to send
the poltergoose back where it belongs.

Shortlisted for the Blue Peter Book Award

What they say about
The POLTERGOOSE

I would give this book 10 out of 10
Victoria Guilder, age 9

A laugh a minute, I couldn't stop turning the pages!
Caroline Holworthy, age 12

I thought this book was excellent, the exciting storyline, the perfect description of the things the goose did and the results.
Carolyn Thomas, age 11

HONK!

I would recommend this to anybody
Simon Ward

The Poltergoose is brilliant!
Sarah Goddard, age 10

A clever, funny story which children will be able to relate to
Alison Broderick, age 11

HONK!

Hilarious.
Times Educational Supplement

The Poltergoose is full of detail and a brilliant book
Mark Middleton

Rib-tickling.
Sunderland Echo

wacky and streetwise.
The Bookseller

I liked the comical storyline
Victoria Walton, age 12

HONK!

A Jiggy McCue Story

The Killer Underpants

Michael Lawrence

1 84121 713 1   £4.99

The underpants from hell – that's what Jiggy
calls them, and not just because they look so
gross. No, these pants are evil. And they're
in control. Of him. Of his life!
Can Jiggy get to the bottom of his problem
before it's too late?

**Winner of the Stockton Children's
Book of the Year Award**

what they say about

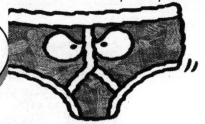

"Fantastic, real and very funny."
Bernard Ashley
Author

"Michael Lawrence digs into your funny bone and does not relinquish his grip until every tickle has been tickled."
Kevin McLaughlin
Teacher

Has irresistible boy appeal.
The Bookseller

Entertaining and original
Booktrust

"The story really made me giggle. A brilliant book to read for everyone!"
Rebecca Moss
Acquila

"Some very funny things happen in this book. It made me laugh out loud."
Elizabeth Law
YARN

This is the funniest book I've ever read.
Teen Titles

Quirky, cheeky fun that children will love.
Books Magazine/
Publishing News

1 84121 752 2   £4.99

Feel like your life has gone down the pan?
Well here's your chance to swap it
for a better one!

When those tempting words appear on the
computer screen, Jiggy McCue just can't resist..
He hits "F for Flush" and...Oh dear.
He really shouldn't have done that. Because
the life he gets in place of his own is a very
embarrassing one – for a boy.

More Red Apples to get your teeth into...

1 84121 435 3   £3.99

Do Not Read This Book by Pat Moon

'Nolly's given me this notebook... I will use it to record my life and secret thoughts...'

Finch lives with her unconventional "girl power" family – a messy, scatty Mum – and a chain-smoking adopted gran, Nolly. Then her mum's new boyfriend starts changing a few things and Finch launches a campaign to get rid of "Action Man". But when she succeeds, Finch finds that she's bitten off more than she can chew.

"A terrific read." *The Guardian*

Shortlisted for the Sheffield Children's Book Award

1 84121 539 2   £4.99

The Salt Pirates of Skegness by Chris d'Lacey

Jason's Aunt Hester is a grouchy old stick.
But a witch? Surely not?
But then, why is there a whole crew of
pirates held prisoner in her cellar...?

Aided by Scuttle, the saltiest, smelliest seadog ever,
Jason sets out to solve the mystery and defeat
the evil Skegglewitch.

Chris d'Lacey's book, *Fly, Cherokee, Fly* was
Highly Commended for the Carnegie Medal.

orchard Red Apples

☐ *The Poltergoose*	Michael Lawrence	1 86039 836 7	£4.99
☐ *The Killer Underpants*	Michael Lawrence	1 84121 713 1	£4.99
☐ *The Toilet of Doom*	Michael Lawrence	1 84121 752 2	£4.99
☐ *The Fire Within*	Chris d'Lacey	1 84121 533 3	£4.99
☐ *The Salt Pirates of Skegness*	Chris d'Lacey	1 84121 539 2	£4.99
☐ *Do Not Read This Book*	Pat Moon	1 84121 435 3	£3.99
☐ *How To Eat Fried Worms*	Thomas Rockwell	1 85213 722 3	£4.99
☐ *How To Fight a Girl*	Thomas Rockwell	1 86039 347 0	£3.99
☐ *How To Get Fabulously Rich*	Thomas Rockwell	1 86039 349 7	£3.99
☐ *What Howls at the Moon in Frilly Knickers*	E.F. Smith	1 84121 808 1	£4.99

Orchard Red Apples are available from all good bookshops,
or can be ordered direct from the publisher:
Orchard Books, PO BOX 29, Douglas IM99 1BQ
Credit card orders please telephone 01624 836000
or fax 01624 837033 or visit our Internet site: www.wattspub.co.uk
or e-mail: bookshop@enterprise.net for details.

To order please quote title, author and ISBN
and your full name and address.
Cheques and postal orders should be made payable to
'Bookpost plc.'
Postage and packing is FREE within the UK
(overseas customers should add £1.00 per book).
Prices and availability are subject to change.

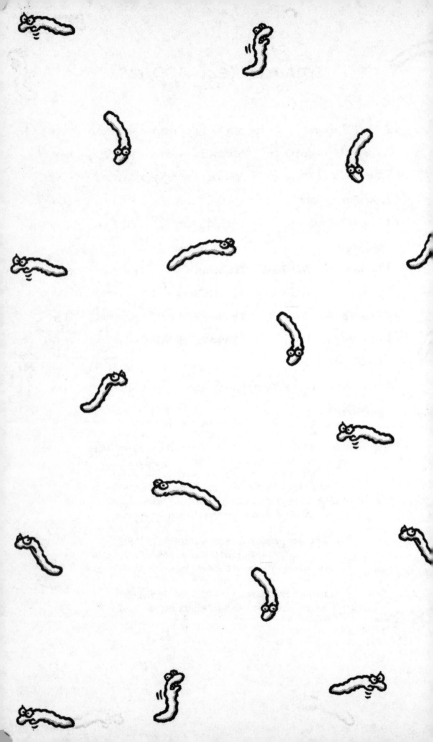

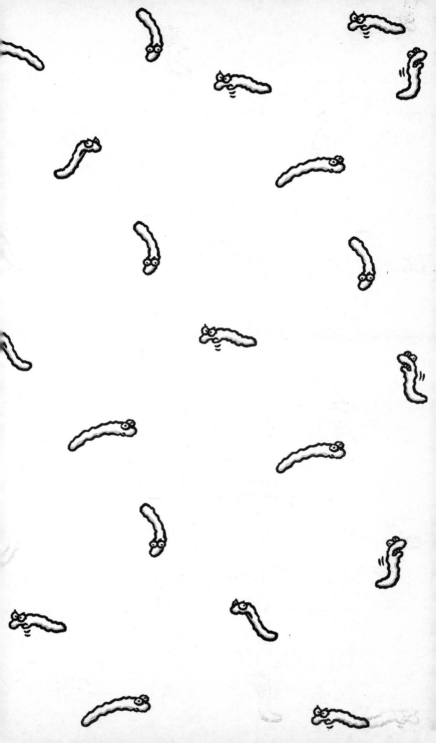